I0822161

Praise for

TARO THE ZEN CAT

"*Taro the Zen Cat* is the embodiment of the question that lives in the silence of every human heart, 'Who am I?' Most of us don't have the courage to even ask the question. Not only does Taro ask the question, but with the help of an extraordinary cast of characters, he shows us that it's possible to answer that most fundamental question that gives being alive its meaning and dignity."

—William *Yoshin Gennan* Jordan, Roshi Emeritus. Abbot, *Gakiji* Hungry Ghost Zen Buddhist Temple, 1994-2014

"You don't have to be a cat lover, or even a Zen lover, to love this book. *Taro the Zen Cat* embodies the universal desire to find one's life's purpose, whatever that may be. The book gently reveals Zen principles with humor, intelligence, and compassion. Most of all, following Taro on his journey is great fun. In this Zen monastery, a cat is accepted on the same terms as any other student, a rat is consumed by resentment, and the birds serve as emissaries to the outside world. The tale works on multiple levels, allowing readers of all ages to absorb the parts that speak to them. It's entertainment for everyone."

—Laurie Horowitz, Writer, Editor, Teacher, Consultant, Westside Writers' Lab

"It is always a pleasure when Jennifer Hunter puts pen to paper. She knows just which words will best weave a vibrant story, make characters come alive as if ready to pounce from the page, especially when they are cats or critters, and guide her reader into new territory with clarity, cunning, and compelling logic. Her mastery of imagination, ideas, and the Zen of awareness make her writing subtle, yet crisp and delicious. I always want more!"

—Diane Curran, Founder, The Marketing Deal. Marketing & Branding Consultant. Podcast Host of *Wow Whispering*

"Taro's is a captivating tale of a spiritual journey and finding one's place. Using traditional Zen training, the reader is lured into a cast of animal and human characters, their families, and transformation. For those of us with a background in this kind of residential training, it is a heart-warming reflection on the role of Zen training and its extension into society. The main character, Taro, is inspirational, yet very much the cat next door. I would recommend this book to anyone."

—Charles *Tenshin* Fletcher, Roshi. Abbot, *Yokoji* Zen Mountain Center Temple. Co-Author of *The Way of Zen*

"Conveying her love and understanding of Zen principles via the natural world tickles the imagination and promotes a sense of tranquility. Jennifer Hunter's miraculous story offers insight to a world that may help others to overcome obstacles in their lives. The narrative is beautifully written and flows like leaves in a stream."

—Ren'e Fedyna, Author of *Dance of the Restless Soul, Dance with the Devil*

"How could you not be totally absorbed by this wonderful story about a ginger cat seeking enlightenment? *Taro the Zen Cat* has quickly become one of my all-time favorite stories and is definitely one that I will read again and again. I found it very uplifting, charming, and delightful. Jennifer Hunter is a brilliant and funny writer and has a very entertaining way of pulling back the curtain into the Zen Buddhist world. You will be entertained regardless of your spiritual path or lack of one. This is a warm and wonderful story that I will treasure for years to come. I'll definitely be giving many copies as Christmas gifts this year. Would love to see this as an animated film!"

—Andrew Thomas Roth, Founder, Bulletproof Your Soul Coaching for Men

"Wow! This is a terrific book! Beautifully written and satisfying to the very end. Taro is darling and a true hero in his attempt to understand enlightenment and reach his purpose. I would love to see where he is now!"

—Jill Jordan, Owner, Portugal Properties

Taro the Zen Cat

JENNIFER J. HUNTER

FROM THE TINY ACORN...
GROWS THE MIGHTY OAK

Taro the Zen Cat

Printed in the United States of America. For information, address
Acorn Publishing, LLC
3943 Irvine Blvd. Ste. 218, Irvine, CA 92602

www.acornpublishingllc.com

Interior design by Kat Ross
Cover design by Damonza

ISBN-13: 979-8-88528-074-7 (hardcover)
ISBN-13: 979-8-88528-073-0 (paperback)
Library of Congress Control Number: 2023912122

To Rev. Bill Yoshin Gennan Jordan, Roshi. I wrote Taro the Zen Cat as my final love letter to Zen and as an acknowledgment for the years of training you freely gave that so positively and profoundly guided and changed my life. My gratitude for who you were to me and all of us at Gakiji is so profound that I stumble on words to express myself. But I remember everything. And your influence and teachings live with me forever.

And to Sumi Goto-Jordan. Thank you for being his wife, his partner, and the light and love of his life. He is lucky to have you. And so am I.

Author's Note

The *Gakiji* Hungry Ghost Zen Buddhist Temple was real. *Gennan* Roshi is also a real person. Roshi closed *Gakiji,* originally known as the Santa Monica Zen Center, many years ago but he still taught for short periods on an individual basis for a while longer.

One day, I asked him if he would take on Taro as his student for the sake of making the book as authentic as possible. He agreed. At that point, I embodied Taro in *dokusan* (private interviews) with Roshi in his home and on the phone. We worked on one *kōan* (Case 23 of the *kōan* collection from the Mumonkan: The Gateless Gate – *Think Neither Good Nor Evil* – in which the words were slightly altered to fit the needs of the story. This is not an uncommon practice). We also had many interactions unrelated to direct *kōan* study. We studied all possible angles of what one would do or say to the other. Dialogues, expressions, stories, responses, interactions, and musings in this book were as true as any possible interaction could be with an authentic Zen Master.

Taro the Zen Cat is a work of fiction based on the facts of the personal experiences I had during my decades of Zen training and practice at *Gakiji*. However, as I continued writing, it occurred to me that over the successive generations, some information had been lost in the transmission of the forms, rituals, and ceremonies belonging to Zen. Many dedications and gathas we chanted in our practice at *Gakiji* have gone unclaimed by any author, to my knowledge. As a result, I am unable to give credit to whomever wrote certain pieces I have quoted in the book. Specifically, these include: the portion of the dedication chanted during *Fusatsu*, the portion of the Meal Gatha chanted during *oryoki*, the Evening Gatha chanted at the end of the last period of *zazen*, and the directives given in *tokudo* (ordination).

I clearly took artistic license with this story. I was ordained in the United States as a Zen Buddhist priest, and only knew myself as *priest*. As far as I know, in the United States, anyone who completed studies that ended in *tokudo* called him or herself a *priest*. But I could be mistaken. I own my own experience.

However, in Taro's story, I chose not to use the term *priest*, but instead opted for the term *monk*. My understanding of the difference between the two words is that a monk is celibate while a Zen priest is not. None of us were, anyway. But for the sake of the story, I chose *monk* because it felt more fitting to the mood and local color of the story. And, most importantly, it's a story. A hero's journey. *Zen* is the outward form Taro chose. Maybe yours is entirely different. Taro can lead you anywhere on your own journey. That's the beauty. Enjoy yourself and thank you for coming along on the ride.

Jennifer J. *Isshin* Hunter, Ph.D.
Cuenca, Ecuador
Visit my website at www.JenniferJHunter.com

Foreword

Jennifer J. Hunter has written a very beautiful and deeply moving account of Zen life under the guidance of a Zen Master, a Roshi. This book gives the reader a profound and accurate experience of what it is like to study in a monastic setting. In doing so, she has hit the mark on what I feel is the future of both Zen Buddhism and spiritual practice in general - the inclusion of all living beings from the greater vantage point of one world, one planet, united in harmony and respect for one another.

She portrays this forest monastic community, including cats, mice, birds, rats, deer, and people, living in harmony amidst their petty jealousies and envies, transcending their differences, coming from a deep realization of our oneness, with deep love and appreciation of our uniqueness.

This book brings to life the longing for meaning and purpose we all face at some point in our lives, and how this challenged cat finds his way and truth for himself. And how we can find our peace and liberation not in separation from our life but in the midst of our own pain and suffering and the pain and suffering of others. By not resisting, denying or suppressing our pain, we allow ourselves to experience it directly without trying or needing to escape from it.

I cried through many parts of the book, reflecting on my experiences at a much earlier time in my life, of the strong disciplined love of community, and the often ruthless compassion of practice with my Zen Master, *Maezumi* Roshi.

D. *Genpo* Merzel, Roshi
Portland, Oregon
Big Mind Zen
https://www.bigmind.org/

CHAPTER *One*

THE SHOPKEEPER RAN out the door, red-faced, jowls quivering. He slammed the broom down on the pebble walkway, missing Taro's tail by a hair. "Get out of here! This food is not for you. Get out! You're fat enough already!"

Sachi, Taro's younger sister by a minute or two, became a blur of gray fur as she sped past him, snatched the burlap bag of food out of his mouth, and headed for safety under a bush. Then she turned and waited for Taro, anxiously scratching the ground as she encouraged him to run faster.

Taro felt a whoosh of air as the broom came down again hard behind him. He tucked his tail in as far as it would go and bolted to safety.

Taro's eyes were wide with fear. "Oh, Sachi! I almost didn't make it!"

Sachi licked her brother's ginger face. "It's okay. Catch your breath. You're safe. Let's just stay here for a while."

Taro panted, "I can't do this. I can't do this anymore!"

"Taro, stop saying that. You can do this. You can. Just calm down. Don't talk right now."

Sachi rubbed her head under her brother's chin. "Just because it's expected of you to provide like this, it doesn't mean it always has to be this way." She already knew how difficult it was for Taro to reconcile their father's and baby brother's deaths. His entire future had instantly changed. The tragedy had occurred in early spring and here it was already the end of the year. But it still felt like yesterday for Taro. Sachi continued to purr and rub under his chin until she felt his body begin to uncoil and relax.

When Taro's breathing slowed to normal, the two cats hunkered down, side by side, under the protection of the bush. They watched the people, dogs, and other cats roaming around the open-air marketplace. Years ago, this addition to their little village had brought the community closer together. There was an open fire pit in the center for cold winter days like today. A food court circled the pit where café owners had placed outdoor tables for their customers. For Sachi, this was as good as handing food directly to her. Once she realized the food was brought outside on plates and put on the tables, she became a master of the grab and go. She was an agile jumper and lightning speed runner.

Taro, on the other hand, lumbered. He couldn't jump high, and his body type was best suited for staying low and picking up scraps dropped on the ground. The shopkeeper had called him *fat*. Sachi thought of him as *dense*. Either way, he was a bottom-dweller and not fit to be the provider his mother expected him to be as her first-born now that Papa was gone.

As Taro and Sachi watched the comings and goings in the marketplace, a prolonged, rich, guttural monotone "*Hōoooo . . .*" caught Taro's attention. Coming from deep within the belly and extending out for as long as possible on a single length of breath, it was contrasted by the sweet jingle of bells. Taro had never heard anything so oddly beautiful. He turned in the direction of these new sounds and waited. Something was coming.

A procession of five monks stopped at a near-by shop. The guttural monotone and the tinkling of bells ceased. Nothing happened. Then, shopkeepers in nearby stores filed into the street, putting their offerings of food into the monks' bowls and money, jewelry or other valuables into the satchels that hung around their necks. The monks waited.

On impulse, Taro said, "Sachi, is it okay if I put some food in their bowls?"

"Sure. I can always get more."

Taro took a tentative step away from the bush, looked in both directions just to be sure, and hesitated. Then, stepping forward more confidently, he approached the lead monk and placed some string beans and a half-eaten baked potato into his bowl.

The monk, wearing a wide brimmed straw hat that obscured his vision except for the ground in front of him, bowed in Taro's direction. Then the monks began to chant several verses of Gratitude and Giving, blessing Taro and all those around him. When they finished, the five monks moved on to the next block, announcing themselves on a continuous vibrant echo of "*Hōoooo* . . ." accompanied by the jingling bells.

"What was that all about, Taro? What just happened?" Sachi asked, glancing between Taro and the backs of the monks who began to turn the corner.

"It was like that monk was waiting for me."

"You think so? I don't understand," Sachi said.

"Me either," Taro said as the last monk faded from his view. "But I felt a connection, almost like a memory I can't quite place."

"But something happened," Sachi said.

"Yeah, something just happened."

"Well, watch me! I can make something happen, too." Her fierce green eyes shining, Sachi jumped onto a nearby table in the open-air marketplace and grabbed the remains of a pork chop from a plate before the diner even knew what had happened.

As the two cats walked home along a dirt road, Taro turned to Sachi. “Let me carry the bag. It’s my job.” He took the burlap out of his sister’s mouth, stopped walking, and sat down. Sachi waited.

“I need to talk about this, Sachi. I hate that I’m not keeping up with you.”

“You don’t have to! We’ve been over this before. I thought we were done talking about this months ago,” Sachi said.

“You’re so good at what you do, you know, getting food for the family. It just keeps reminding me of what a failure I am. I can’t see my way through Mama’s expectations, and I know I can’t go on much longer like this, barely outrunning the shopkeepers.”

“What are you saying, Taro?” Sachi tasted the fear at the edge of her words.

“I’m saying I need to find my own place in the world. You’ve found yours. Now I need to find mine.”

Taro and Sachi shared a secret. A lie, to be honest. But thinking of it as a secret softened the edge for Taro enough to allow him to live with the hard truth. Everything Sachi snatched off the plates of unsuspecting diners, she gave to Taro to take home to Mama and their two other sisters. Mama never suspected, assuming her beautiful Taro was responsible for the livelihood of their family.

Ever since Taro’s father and only brother, Shiro, were killed by an out-of-control horse last spring, Taro had struggled. He jumped between rage and grief. He couldn’t provide for the family like his late father. After all, he wasn’t his father, and he didn't want to be. And he certainly wasn’t anything like his sister. Sachi had the gift of grab. No one else could do what she did. Even their father couldn’t have snatched so much meat on such a short stroll through the village marketplace.

At the time of their deaths, Taro’s mother, Reiko, looked to

Taro, her eldest, to keep the family going. It was tradition. But Taro feared the bustle of the marketplace. He was not agile enough, and he worried someone might trample him. Accidents happened. He was more aware of that than anyone.

Taro hated being shouted at by the storekeepers and diners. He couldn't grab a morsel of food without someone seeing him do it. Unlike Sachi, Taro was unfit for this type of activity, and he knew it. But the family's hunger drove him out to the marketplace every day. He watched food come and go, but he lacked the nerve or the agility to make a snatch. He only ended up with what remained in the breadbaskets after the customers left. Pathetic. It was bad enough that his family was grieving without having them go hungry, too.

Earlier in the year, a week after Taro's father and brother had been killed, Taro was wandering alone in the marketplace when he saw a gray velvet bag on the ground near a table. He snatched it up and ran under his favorite hiding bush where he examined the bag in private. Inside were eight shiny black buttons studded with rhinestones. Oh! These buttons were beautiful. His mother would like them. They would sparkle in the light whenever she held them up. Finally, he had something more than stale bread to offer her. A gift to help his mother feel better. He was so excited, he forgot why he was in the marketplace and went home without any food.

"Mama, look. I brought you a present," Taro said, pushing the bag forward.

Reiko opened the bag. Taro waited for her to look up and smile.

"Taro!" his mother hissed. "These are buttons. They won't feed the family."

Taro lowered his eyes, unable to look at his mother's face. He had failed her again, and was grateful that Sachi, who had been there to witness his encounter, had the decency to turn away.

Taro silently left the house, feeling shame and embarrassment by his mother's reaction. Sachi followed him out.

"I can help you," she said once she knew they wouldn't be overheard.

"What do you mean? What can you do?"

"Come here." She walked over to a nearby tree and dug near the roots. She brought out a burlap bag. Inside were a piece of fish, a chicken breast, and three rice balls.

"Why is it hidden there? It's all dirty," Taro said.

"We can wash it off. You give the food to Mama. Everyone's hungry, so take it. Say it's from you."

Taro knew exactly what Sachi was proposing. "You want me to lie to Mama that I was the one who got this food."

"She expects the food to come from you. There's no other way. It's either that, or you figure out how to do it yourself, Taro. We can't just live on bread. But I can help you."

"But it's not your responsibility."

"You're missing the point. It's not about me. It's much bigger than me or you. It's about our family," Sachi said.

He knew her loyalty to the family was her deepest virtue. She always said she did not need to fight for any recognition of her skills. She did not want the credit. Her offer to Taro was the only way she knew to contribute to the family and to protect their mother from the truth, even though it meant lying. If Mama were to find out Taro wasn't the eldest she thought or expected him to be, it would be too much for her. Sachi needed to keep their mother safe from any more devastating news.

"So? Taro? Are you going to give the food to Mama?"

In the silence of his next breath, the lie between Taro and Sachi was born.

Taro fell victim to his life being dictated by circumstances he believed were beyond his control. He lived in what felt like an ever-narrowing tube, unable to turn in any direction. Yet, had he been able to look beyond himself, he would have seen that

Sachi's skills went unrecognized and, therefore, unappreciated. Even though she never indicated any need for acknowledgment, ultimately, he didn't see how her life fulfilled her either. He never believed she would have been completely satisfied if all she did was give him food to take home to their mother for the rest of their lives. There was so much more she could offer.

Taro did not know or understand how to change his circumstances. But it was something he desperately wanted. To have at least some choice in the matter. He, of course, always thanked Sachi for everything she did for him. Every time Taro did this, Sachi playfully pounced on him. It felt to her like wrestling with a big, squishy puffer ball.

"Gratitude's great, Taro, but it ain't yummy like a hot dog," Sachi would always say. "Besides, it doesn't matter who gets the food, as long as we have something to eat. Just keep taking it to Mama." This was Sachi's way. To work in the shadows.

"Come on, Taro. I know it's been hard, but we must keep going. I can show you how it's done. Come on," Sachi encouraged.

But Taro never took her up on her offer.

Yet claiming Sachi's catch as his own became more and more shameful for Taro. Her kindhearted intentions made him feel even worse about the lie and about himself. If he couldn't provide daily meals to the family on his own, what then was he good for in life? He felt inadequate. But he did feel grateful. Because if it hadn't been for Sachi, the family would have starved.

Taro's was now a family of five: himself, his mother Reiko, and the three sisters – Sachi, Nori, and Mika. Of all of them, Sachi had a unique gift. When she was on the hunt for food, she knew where to look, which people to avoid, who were easy targets, and when to make her move. She was smart and infinitely patient, almost as if she willed the food to her. Whatever Sachi wanted, she was guaranteed to have in the burlap bag that Taro carried for her every day to and from the village marketplace.

Sachi looked exactly like her mother. Long dark gray fur and fierce, sparkling green eyes. Her sister Nori had medium-length, lighter gray fur and amber eyes. Quiet and demure, she preferred to stay close to Mama and Mika. Mama needed all the help she could get with Mika, and Nori gladly assisted in Mika's care whenever she could. "Mama, how can I help you?" was something Nori asked her mother all day, every day.

Mika was a long-haired tortoiseshell tabby, a mixture of her mother and father, and the smallest of the litter. She had grown into a gentle but rather dim cat. She would forget where she was going or what she was doing. She would have forgotten to eat if not for Mama or Nori placing the food directly in front of her and staying with her until she finished. No one knew why Mika was the way she was.

Once, when Mika was about four months old, she was chasing a butterfly in the field next to their home. Following the fluttering creature, she just wandered off. Frantic, everyone spread out until Taro finally spotted her, days later, sitting atop the roof of a shoe repair store on the edge of town, looking up at the sky. It wasn't easy to get her down, mainly because Taro had no idea how to get up to her on the roof. He made several attempts to hoist himself up, but always landed on his back on the ground. Mika, in her own world, was more interested in looking at the footprints of birds in the sky. Finally, the kind owner of the shop heard the commotion, got a ladder, and rescued the little tortie tabby. Mika didn't even know to put up a fuss when the man reached for her. Taro carried Mika home by the scruff of her neck like a newborn. It was the only way.

From then on, Mama and Nori never let Mika out of their sight. She required full time help and supervision.

And then there was Taro. He was a long-haired ginger who looked exactly like their father, only much larger. Of all the siblings in the litter, he was the one whose life had changed the most by the family's tragic loss, having been so quickly thrown into the unwanted role of provider.

Taro's family lived on the outskirts of the village in an abandoned farmhouse about half a mile from the edge of the forest. Taro loved everything about his home, especially the spacious field next door for running and playing. The farmhouse allowed them to lounge or explore for long periods of time. The family usually stayed beneath the farmhouse together in the hot summer months because it was cooler. Best of all, no one bothered them there. They roamed throughout the house wherever or whenever they chose. They had each other, which meant they still had everything.

"Taro," his mother called out. "We're going upstairs to the living room. Would you go out and find some kindling so we can have a little heat tonight in the fireplace? I would love for us to be able to welcome in a toasty New Year."

Taro, grateful she hadn't asked for more food, immediately trotted off in search of kindling.

New Year's Eve was cold and windy. Taro kept his paws moving on the frost-encrusted dirt as he made his way up to the edge of the forest and entered. Here, he would be able to collect some dry kindling and run back home to his family. Usually, he didn't venture this far out, but tonight was different. Soon it would be the beginning of a new year. And for that reason, he had given himself permission to wander out beyond his usual limits.

Taro immediately adjusted to the darkness of the forest. Fully alert, he felt bold and excited. His golden eyes turned into satin saucers, and his whiskers spiked out and forward, allowing him to creep deeper and deeper into the shadows with ease. Every smell, every sensation, every sound immediately felt familiar to Taro. Except for one.

He noticed the forest was blanketed by a haunting sound. Not quite sure what this oddly melodious vibration might be, Taro went on full alert. Yet, it too, held an ancient memory he couldn't quite grasp. His fluffy, ginger body puffed up as large as it could go. Slowly creeping forward, eyes wide, he stared ahead with his head slightly lowered. His ears flattened and his tail swished from side to side as he edged his way toward the sound.

CHAPTER *Two*

THE MAIN GATE to the *Gakiji* Hungry Ghost Zen Buddhist Temple was shut tight. At this hour, no one would be entering the Temple. The candlelit midnight ceremony of *Fusatsu,* in which the monks renewed their vows, neared an end. This ceremony of atonement and purification, passed down over thousands of years, had been led by *Gennan* Roshi for decades, and would continue into infinity. Tonight it held a special significance, being the eve of a new year.

The rhythmic, monosyllabic chanting mesmerized Taro, transporting him back to a life he couldn't quite locate in his mind. He had found his way to the main Temple gate just in time to hear a monk's final, lone chant:

"The first day of the New Year is auspicious. Make your intentions for the New Year. Open to the sheer beauty and possibility of this moment . . ."

Taro stopped breathing. His fur was standing on end. Those words, chanted on clouds of incense, settled upon him like a familiar, delicate hug. *Auspicious, intentions, possibility.* He wondered what they could mean for him. He took a deep breath and moved, ever slightly, toward the Temple's old wooden gate.

Suddenly, a small, dry twig cracked under his weight,

shaking off the hypnotic effect of the chanting. Taro panicked, not knowing how long he had been listening. Moving quickly, he gathered as many twigs as he could and shot out of the forest toward home.

When Taro finally returned home, he found his mother pacing. He deposited the sticks on the floor.

"Taro! Thank goodness! Where have you been? I've been so worried," his mother said.

Dropping the sticks into the traditional open pit fireplace, Reiko lit one and waited for the others to catch. The fire ignited quickly and began to warm the room. She beckoned Taro over and started licking him. "What's that smell all over you, Taro?" she asked.

Taro didn't know what it was. It must have been from those soft clouds that came up over the Temple's gate.

Despite the soothing effect the incense could have had, Taro's mind and body remained restless throughout the remainder of the evening and into the early morning of the first day of the New Year.

"Sachi," Taro whispered. "I need to go somewhere. Can you go to the marketplace alone today? I'm not sure how long I'll be gone."

"Yeah, sure, Taro," Sachi said as she stretched, yawned, and rolled away from him.

More than anything, Taro wanted to get back to the forest and return to the Temple.

In daylight, the forest looked different to Taro. It had come alive with creatures who were making their way, foraging for their morning meals. He saluted a young hawk as it circled overhead. The hawk angled its wings in greeting. Taro moved confidently, feeling free and alive. After so long, happiness felt wholly new to him.

There was a thick cluster of sugar maple trees right outside the Temple's main gate, which was still closed. Offering perfect branches for him to climb, Taro clawed his way up through their maze and settled in a comfortable spot that gave him a grand overview of the Temple grounds. And then he waited.

Soon, Taro saw several monks depart the Temple through the front door, carrying boxes, brooms, and rakes in their hands. They began methodically sweeping away the snow and raking, placing dead branches and twigs in the boxes, rearranging rocks and stones. Then more raking. And then more sweeping. They did not speak or look at one another, yet they worked together seamlessly, flowing like water. To Taro, this gracefulness was cat-like, and he immediately thought of Sachi and began to purr. He was awakened from his dreamy state when he heard a small bell struck twice. *Ching-ching*. The monks gathered their tools and boxes and returned to the Temple.

Three birds descended upon a nearby branch, but Taro stayed rooted to the sugar maple. Two were cardinals. One male and the other a female. The male's crimson beauty against the stark, frosty gray background was stunning. The female's reddish crest and fawn-colored feathers with bold hits of red throughout her body were beautiful to Taro. The other bird, larger in size, was a red-winged blackbird. His feathers were black as oil, and he sported puffed-up, bright red epaulets with yellow wing bars underneath. Facing Taro, he sat on the branch with his tail feathers flared and wings held away from his body. He looked formidable. The two cardinals flanked him on either side. All three inspired awe in Taro. He had never been as close to a bird before without the urge to chase it away.

Not knowing what to expect, he took a chance and asked them, "What is this place?"

The blackbird, Hiroto, said, "This is the *Gakiji* Hungry Ghost Zen Buddhist Temple. Men and women come from all over the country to train and practice Zen here."

"Zen? What is Zen?" Taro asked.

"Zen is the realization of your life moment by moment, lived just as it is, without any added thoughts, opinions, or commentary," he continued.

"*Gennan* Roshi calls Zen a direct experience of reality," the female cardinal, Remi, said.

"*Gennan*? Who is *Gennan*?" asked Taro.

"It's *Gennan* Roshi. That's his title. Never call him *Gennan*. It's not right, but just using Roshi is ok," Remi continued.

"Oh. I'm sorry. Who is *Gennan* Roshi?"

"He's the head of *Gakiji*. The Abbot. The Temple's been in the forest for longer than we've been alive," the scarlet male cardinal, Genji, said. "Roshi has been here twenty, fifty, or maybe even one or two hundred years. We know time by the seasons, but I've lost track."

"A long time, anyway. So how do you know so much about Zen?" Taro asked.

All three birds chirped and whistled over one another. "We were born in the forest and the monastery has always been a part of us. Every Sunday, talks are given to encourage and help the monks understand. We come to the maple trees to listen and learn. Sometimes Roshi even gives informal talks, just walking around. We've grown up with Roshi's training and his monks," Hiroto said.

"Why study Zen? What's the point?"

"Roshi would say to experience freedom from suffering," Remi said.

"Yeah! And that helps you in becoming less miserable and unhappy," said Genji.

"Exactly," said Remi. "When you can be with life on life's terms, your capacity to manage yourself with emotions like upset or grief, hatred or anger, becomes greater."

"Even though sometimes you're still unhappy and cranky, or you hate what you're doing. It can happen." Genji shrugged his wings.

"I still don't understand," said Taro. "Go back to the part

about becoming less miserable and unhappy. How does that work?"

Hiroto continued, "The training is expansive. Boundless, really. Over time, with practice and *Gennan* Roshi's help and guidance, students come to appreciate a spiritual awakening that influences their every breathing moment."

"Hey! I've heard Roshi say a million times that talking about Zen deadens it," Remi said, flapping her wings. "Why are we still talking?"

"Zen is beyond words and letters! You see? There's really nothing more to say after all, kitty cat!" chirped Genji.

Hiroto tilted his head at his companions and continued patiently, "The monks sit in a room called the *zendo*. Over time, they cultivate a discipline that becomes highly focused as ours has to be when we're foraging for beetles and bugs to supplement our winter meals."

"Yes! And to help us out, Roshi and his monks offer birdseed to us and everyone in the forest during the winter months. See over there?" Genji said, lifting a wing. "They keep boxes filled for us in the months that are harder to find food. Like now."

Remi added, "And every spring, after the baby animals have been born, *Gennan* Roshi performs an Animal Blessing ceremony for all of us."

"Yes, the monks are very kind in that way," said Hiroto. "But you see . . . what did you say your name was?"

"Oh, sorry, my name is Taro."

"Well, then, Taro. Please forgive our rudeness in not introducing ourselves properly. This is Remi, and her male companion is Genji," the blackbird said as he passed a broad wing in each of their directions. "And I," he said, returning the wing to his chest and bowing his head slightly, "I am Hiroto. We are pleased to make your acquaintance."

Taro was taken aback. For some reason, he had never thought of birds as having names. "Why, thank you. It's nice to meet you, too," he said, raising a paw and hoping it wouldn't look aggressive. Then, he asked, "Is this Zen thing hard to do?"

"It depends, but, probably. Actually, definitely, yes. Roshi trains his students with the kind wisdom of the Buddha and the nobility and rigor of a samurai warrior," Hiroto said.

"In other words, he's demanding and intense. At least, that's what I would say about him," Remi added.

"But he's a really nice guy! He yells sometimes, though," said Genji.

"What are you talking about?" Remi said. "He doesn't yell. He expresses himself loudly and passionately!"

"That's called yelling!"

"He wants to make sure you understand. It's hardly yelling! You're yelling!"

"No, I'm not! I . . ."

"Stop it, you two!" Hiroto said, flapping his wings several times to settle them back in.

Taro stared at the birds. They were more dramatic and excitable than anyone he had ever known.

"You can think of Zen as more of a way of being," said Hiroto.

"Yes! There's no escaping your physical existence. Roshi talks about Zen as being practical, firmly fixed to the earth," said Remi.

"Like, it's not woo-woo up in the sky stuff," Genji offered.

"But how does that make me feel less miserable?" Taro asked.

"Right now, you think you know who you are and how your mind works," said Hiroto, thrusting his beak close to Taro's face. "Yes?"

"Haha, that ain't it. I love this part!" Genji jumped up and down on a branch, knocking off some snow.

Taro slowly pulled his face back, keeping an eye on the blackbird's beak.

"With Roshi's guidance and training, his students learn how to become masters of their own minds," said Remi.

"I still don't understand," Taro replied.

"Say your mind is like a strong ox," explained Hiroto. "Rather than being pulled along by this ox, living at the effect of whatever your mind wants or thinks, you'll eventually learn to ride the ox and be in control of your thoughts and actions."

"Until there's no ox left at all! It happens. Just wait!" said Genji.

Hiroto sighed and continued patiently, "It's called gaining mastery over your own mind. For example, men and women sometimes come to the Temple because they don't quite understand what their lives are meant to be. They might feel lost or unsatisfied. Incomplete in some way. They know something is missing. Once they gain some mastery, they learn to appreciate their lives. And, with proper work and guidance, they discover meaning and purpose. It takes time, though. At least as long as it takes the students to become monks. So we're talking years. That's how long it takes. But sometimes it's really quite profound what happens."

"I need to get in there to find out for myself," said Taro, his curiosity piqued.

"Don't climb over the gate just because you can. You must announce yourself properly. That way, Roshi will take you seriously. Don't try to sneak inside," Remi advised.

Taro's whiskers began to twitch. Waves of electricity rolled through his body as tiny hairs prickled along his undercoat and up his spine. Something felt utterly familiar in all that was strange around him.

"You're a cat. Cats bring luck and good fortune to Temples," Hiroto said. "But remember this, Taro. No matter what we just said, don't get any weird ideas about *Gennan* Roshi, or you will be very disappointed. He's a human being. And that's where the magic is. Not in your projection of who you think he should be." With that, the birds flew away.

And without hesitation, Taro chose.

CHAPTER *Three*

SOMEWHERE BETWEEN THE Temple gate and home, Taro's nerves slipped. His Reasonable Mind wagged an admonishing finger in his head. *What's wrong with you thinking you can just up and leave your family like that? It's insane! And selfish. Just go back to what you know and everything will be fine. Your purpose is to take the food to your mother and your family. Just do that and that's it. It's an easy life. Don't try to be a big shot. Forget about doing anything else.*

But Taro fought against his Reasonable Mind. He wanted to find his authentic purpose in life. To find something to do that he loved and was good at. To make a contribution. Everyone deserved that.

What happens when you fail? Because you know you will! And this Zen stuff sounds fishy. You don't know anything about it. It's too risky. Taro's Reasonable Mind kept going and going. After all, this Mind protected him and allowed him to survive in the world. It was the Mind's job, but still . . . *Tell me! After you fail, where will you go? What will you do? You can't go home. You'd be a laughing stock. A humiliation to your mother. Your sisters would never respect you again, certainly not Sachi.*

"No! Stop it!" Taro cried out, bringing his paws to his head.

In that moment, he felt overwhelmed by fear and doubt. He could have easily given in to his Reasonable Mind.

But Taro was also sick of this internal struggle. So far, he had always lost the battle and wound up right back where he'd started.

Taro! Listen to me! Be a good boy. Just go home. It's safe and predictable there. You're taken care of and you're with your family. If you think some human will help you, you're crazy. You don't even know who he is or if he even exists! And who are these birds with names? Ridiculous! Go home! Sachi will find something extra special nice for you tonight as a reward for doing what's right.

Sachi! Just the thought of her taking care of him reflected all his regrets, all his disappointments in himself. The times he had given up on himself, his excuses, how small and safe he had kept his life.

Stop Taro, stop! Stay with what you know! You're making a big mistake!

But Taro knew. This time, it would be a much bigger mistake if he didn't go.

As Taro approached his home, he saw Sachi digging in the backyard. A large burlap bag was on the ground next to her. It looked full. He walked over to her. "What's in the bag?"

Sachi moved closer. "Where have you been?"

Taro started pawing at the bag. When it fell open, he was shocked. "Did you get all this food today? By yourself?"

"It was nothing. I was in and out of the marketplace in no time. I could have gotten more, but . . ." Sachi shrugged.

"Hey, is there any meat or maybe some fish in there? I've been walking for a long time, and I'm hungry."

"Paws off, Taro!" Sachi spit back as she swiped the bag away from him. "Answer my question first. Where have you been?" She felt uneasy. Something was about to happen, she was sure.

Taro sighed. Just looking at the enormous bag of food Sachi had brought home showed her skill as a provider. She didn't need him. In fact, he knew he slowed her down. Got in her way. Which made it even worse. He couldn't put the conversation off any longer.

"It's time for me to go. I have to find my purpose for being in the world, find a direction for myself. I need to go away, because I won't ever find the answer here."

"What are you talking about? What do you mean?" Sachi asked, her sense of unease deepening.

"My life has to be about something more than following you around in the marketplace and lying to Mama for the rest of our lives."

"No, Taro, please. Don't say that. You don't have to go. Find something else to do! This is working for us. The food is handled. I'm telling you, it's working!" Sachi cried out.

"But it's not working for me."

Sachi looked at her brother. She had always known Taro was not suited for the role he was thrust into. He could barely jump without falling back. He could never get good lift-off and certainly wasn't fleet of foot. It was painful for Sachi to watch. It wasn't that there was anything wrong with Taro. Far from it. He just wasn't fit for the role. And yes, she always worried that maybe one day he would get hurt, or worse, caught.

Sachi didn't know what he meant when he talked about leaving, but she had to admit that anything would be better than the life he was living now. In her heart, she knew her brother needed to figure out his inner conflict, even if it meant going away. But that same heart was breaking because she loved him so much.

"You know, I don't know if Mama is going to be able to handle this. She might become hysterical. She will be afraid that there is no one to provide for the family," Sachi said in an attempt to stall the information she knew was coming.

Taro's Reasonable Mind sprang into action. *Listen to Sachi. She's right. This is going to kill your mother. Is that what you want?*

"More than ever, Sachi, I . . ."

"Because," Sachi said desperately, cutting Taro off, "Mama may very well draw a line in the sand and you won't have a place in this family to come back to once you leave. Did you think about that?"

Taro let out a long breath and cast his eyes downward. "I don't want to think about anything anymore. I've already thought too much. I have to do something different with my life. I have to. And I guess there's a price for that."

"Yeah, a really high price, Taro. Like the price of losing your family!" Sachi cried.

"Will you support me when I tell Mama tonight?"

"I don't want to!"

"Please, Sachi. I just want this chance. I know it's a big gamble that you don't understand, but please. . ."

"Well, I don't have a choice, do I! If this is what you need, then I'll help you. But I still don't understand why you have to leave. I love you so much! I can't imagine my life without you here."

Taro placed his forehead on his sister's. "Thank you."

"Where are you going?" she asked.

"To a Zen Buddhist Temple in the forest."

Taro's mother's angry hisses and yowls were agonizing and went on and on throughout the night like sirens endlessly rolling through the streets of the village. Taro sat on the dirt floor in front of her with his head lowered. Sachi stood attentively off to the side just in case she had to rush in to help either one. Nori huddled in the corner, holding onto little Mika, who was playing with her tail.

Yet despite Taro's suffering, he was at last free from the lie. And he was grateful Sachi had understood his need enough to accept a new role for herself, recognized by Mama as the oldest and now the family's provider.

Yet his mother's grief and anguish were so profound, she told Taro the minute he walked out the door, she would banish him from the family, and he would become dead to her. But Taro knew he would think of his mother and sisters every day and send them prayers wrapped in his love and some of that great smelly stuff that came out of the Temple in wispy clouds. He wasn't dead. In fact, he felt as if he had just come alive. He had taken his first step. A step away from all he knew. A leap of faith.

CHAPTER Four

THE WINTER MONTHS in the north of the country were often harsh. This year there had been heavy snowfall and the temperatures had not looked kindly on warm-blooded creatures. Taro's hair had grown thick, but he still found himself shivering to generate even more heat in his large body as he approached the old wooden Temple gate.

Looking around, Taro finally realized he had to pull the cord attached to a bell to announce his arrival. He pulled the cord twice and waited until he heard crunching footsteps approach the gate. Swinging the gate open slowly, a bald head presented itself. Looking around from side to side, the monk seemed perplexed.

Taro called out, "Down here, sir!"

Lowering his gaze, the monk saw an enormous, fluffy, long-haired ginger cat sitting on the ground, looking up at him with earnest eyes.

The monk smiled, feeling a blessing was about to be bestowed upon him. Cats always heralded good luck.

"How can I help you, Ginger Cat?" the monk asked.

"My name is Taro. I have come to ask permission to enter the monastery and train with Roshi. I want to become a monk," Taro said.

The monk shook his head in disbelief. "Just jump over the gate and hang out for a while if you want. We've never taken a cat as a student before. And I'm sure no cat monks," he said as he shut the gate.

But Taro remembered what the birds had told him. Cats were good luck to the Temple monks, but that luck might not be enough to get him formally through the gate. He grabbed the cord and rang the bell again several times.

Eventually, Taro again heard the monk's approaching footsteps. The gate slowly swung open.

"You again," he said.

Taro insisted, "I want to train with Roshi!"

The monk just shook his head, saying, "The *zendo's* full, and he's not accepting any more students. Roshi isn't ordaining any more monks. Absolutely no cats. Never heard of such a thing!" And he shut the gate again.

Breathing so heavily that large puffs of condensation came billowing out his mouth and nostrils, Taro started to sharpen his claws on the Temple gate but thought better of it. Instead, he grabbed the cord again and yanked on it, wildly ringing the bell over and over and over again until he heard footsteps.

Before the monk even opened his mouth, Taro said, "I am here because I want to train with Roshi!"

The monk said, "This is fruitless, but I'll take a note to him. Just don't expect anything to come of this." And the Temple gate was shut again, this time more forcefully.

In the early evening, the monk returned with a written response from Roshi. *"NO!"*

Taro said, "Let me see that." And sure enough, there was Roshi's stinging response. At least Taro assumed so. He couldn't read. But now, emboldened by the fear he would never be admitted, Taro asked the monk if he had a pencil, which the monk eventually found in his jacket pocket.

Taro didn't know how to write either, so he asked the monk to respond back. Taro wanted his desire to train with Roshi to be known and recorded. Taro asked Roshi to please reconsider his request, vowing to stay at the gate all night, into the next day, and longer, if the need arose.

Even though the monk would never dare show it, he had the smallest of soft spots for Taro. Because he was a cat, the monk thought there might still be some blessing afforded to him. On behalf of the entire Temple, of course. But to mask this desire, the monk shouted, "Hey! This is ridiculous. But I'll take the request to Roshi one last time! And because it's getting late, you can shelter yourself over there." He pointed to what resembled a small, but formal outside waiting room, which faced the main gate. "Here. Here's some bread. In the meantime, quietly wait there in *zazen*. You've heard of it, yes? *Zazen?*"

"No, not exactly," Taro said.

Oh brother, lamented the monk to himself, rolling his eyes. "*Zazen* is sitting still and being at attention. Easier said than done. Anyway, you sit with your back straight, hands, well, paws in your case, together, legs crossed. Your back ones, those ones right there, eyes lowered, and watch your breath. When thoughts or feelings come up, go back to your breath. Try to remain neutral, which of course means you won't. Sorry, that's life. Anyway, just sit there, at least in a *zazen* posture, and don't bother me anymore. Stop ringing the bell. Eat the bread. And be quiet!"

With that, the Temple gate was shut in Taro's face once again.

Zazen was not difficult for Taro. In fact, he felt it would be easy because, as a cat, he was a natural. He knew he could sit contentedly inside the little room that faced the Temple gate for a very long time, especially when imagining the gate as the door to a large pizza oven.

But, as it turned out, the night was not so easy. Unrelenting waves of doubt and fear churned in Taro's belly and washed up over his body. It had never occurred to him that he could be declined at the gate. Even when he heard the monks start their eerie chanting and the mysterious, wonderful smells of the incense wafted up and over the Temple gate, Taro found only minimal comfort. He was too distracted. He had left his family for this. He had made his choice to come to *Gakiji* Temple, which now felt immature and impulsive. But he could not return home. The next time the Temple gate opened, Taro's future would be handed to him. He would either have the opportunity to train and become a monk of *Gennan* Roshi's and find his purpose, or he would become a homeless village stray.

Sitting outside the Temple gate in the middle of the night in the little box of a room in the freezing cold, Taro tried to slow his thoughts and feelings. He narrowed his eyes and started to purr. However, his fluttering throat sounds were not the result of contentment, but the tug-of-war between hope and fear.

Before the moon had gone down between the branches of the cluster of sugar maples that stood outside the monastery, the Temple gate opened, and the bald-headed monk stuck his head out once again. He looked at Taro. "You're still here. Well, get up and follow me. You can wash the pots and pans and sweep the floors. Talk to the head cook in the kitchen over there to your right. He might even give you something to eat if you ask him. No promises."

And this time, the Temple gate shut behind Taro as he walked through.

Shortly after Taro was escorted into *Gakiji,* the three birds lighted again on the branches of the sugar maple. Looking down upon the Temple grounds, Remi pointed her wing. "Hey, will you look at that? The cat actually made it through the gate."

The birds remained perched on the maple tree branches, watching through the large windows into the kitchen until Taro finished sweeping the floor.

"Wow, that's wild. Big broom, little cat," Genji quipped.

"This is going to be fun. Let's see how Taro becomes a Zen cat," Hiroto said as the three flew off again, chirping and whistling excitedly.

Twin buck fawns, Ben and Ren, stood below the sugar maples and listened to the birds talk. They had heard the birds in their first encounter with Taro when they had explained the meaning of Zen to him. Now, Taro was past the gate.

Ren turned to his brother. "You know, I could be a Zen student, too. I could study with *Gennan* Roshi."

"You? A Zen student? Are you kidding? There's no Zen in your future," his brother Ben said, shaking his head.

"Why not?"

"Because you can't even sit through one of Roshi's informal dharma talks in the forest without wandering off and fiddling with something unimportant."

"I could change. It would be fun to work with Roshi," said Ren.

"There's nothing fun about Roshi's training, unless you like being sent through a woodchipper. Tell the truth, Ren. You really need a compelling reason to start this practice."

"I think Taro is brave for doing this," said Ren.

"Yeah, Taro is. But you? Stay on this side of the Temple gate," said his twin.

For weeks, Taro stayed in the kitchen and no one talked to him. At least it was warm when the fires were stoked under the large cauldrons used to heat the water for the rice and vegetables. But there was little else good about being in the kitchen, as far as he could see.

If I had wanted to sweep floors, I could have stayed home with a smaller broom. And if cats are so special, how come no one even talks to me? I'm just more free labor to these eggheads. And the head cook? He's so grumpy. Does he think I'm going to steal an extra grain of rice or something? And where's Roshi and all this samurai training and wisdom stuff? I would hate to be those birds if they were lying to me. . .

On and on Taro's thoughts went as he swept the floors and washed the pots and pans, day after day, over and over again, from 4:00 a.m. until 9:00 p.m. Only his desire to train with Roshi kept him there. That, and his enormous fear of failure and being booted out to the street.

One day, after what could have been a month but felt like an eternity, *Daishin,* the head monk and Roshi's attendant, made an announcement in the kitchen. He said that evening there would be a formal Entering Ceremony in the Buddha Hall. The head cook was to prepare for an elaborate Tea Ceremony.

Daishin approached Taro in the back of the kitchen. "Taro," he said, "it is proper for you to bring a gift to offer *Gennan* Roshi to show your appreciation." This was *Daishin's* way of telling Taro that the Entering Ceremony was for him!

Finally! Step on my tail, I must be dreaming. Taro was overjoyed. *Gennan* Roshi was really real! Taro would finally meet him, be given his own seat in the *zendo,* and train together with the other monks. Now all he had to do was find a gift befitting a Roshi. Obviously, it couldn't be something he took from the kitchen. No, it had to be something fresh and unique. Something of his own doing.

While the head cook was overseeing his servers offering the early evening meal to the monks in the *zendo* that evening, Taro crept out the back door. Suddenly, a little gray field mouse ran out in front of him. Taro pounced. The little mouse lay still on the ground.

Taro had seen the monks always offering up prayers of gratitude for all the labors that went into a meal. Even though the mouse wasn't going to become a meal for either Roshi or Taro, he offered up his own prayer of gratitude for its life, telling the mouse it had not lived in vain. After all, it would soon become a very important and significant offering to *Gennan* Roshi.

As Taro picked up the small, limp creature by its tail, he noticed a tuft of unruly white hair atop its head. "Oh, look! You're so special," said Taro to the still mouse. "You're an excellent Roshi gift. I have to hide you so no one can get to you before I offer you tonight." He found the perfect spot outside on top of a small pool of frozen water. He covered his gift with leaves and twigs to keep it safe and protected until later that evening.

Well after the sun had set, and after one period of evening *zazen* was completed, the kitchen servers offered the monks tea with one cookie each on a saucer. This was very special, as cookies were only served on exceptional occasions. Welcoming in a novitiate was one of them.

Before Taro made his way to the threshold of the Buddha Hall for the ceremony, he rushed out to get the little mouse to offer up to Roshi. Upon seeing the cold, now stiff little body, he apologized for having killed it and thanked the mouse again for allowing its life to be of service. He also sent up a prayer of thanks to his mother. And he bowed deeply to Sachi in thanks and gratitude for allowing him this opportunity, whatever it may be. These prayerful acts surprised him. He hadn't even started Zen training and yet he was acting in a more expansive and appreciative way. At least Taro thought that was Zen and what he was supposed to do. He wasn't really sure.

The evening of Taro's Entering Ceremony, candles lit the large Buddha Hall. Incense, having been burned in this Hall for centuries, permeated the space, living and breathing in the walls, the cushions, and the monks' robes. Everything smelled holy, pure, and sacred. It was one of Taro's favorite rooms in the Temple's complex.

Gennan Roshi sat on the traditional high seat, flanked to his right by *Daishin,* his attendant, and the second most senior monk to his left. A *ryoban,* or row of senior monks, was formed on the floor below Roshi. In an equal number, their mats and cushions were positioned directly across from one another, leaving sufficient space to walk right through the middle to approach Roshi directly. And from the *ryoban,* fanning out to the walls all around in impeccable order, were cushions on mats where the remaining monks stood, waiting for Taro to enter. There were so many monks at *Gakiji,* that it was impossible to count the many rows filling the space of the Buddha Hall. All that mattered was Taro's heart was as full as the Buddha Hall itself.

The intense resonance of the *taiko* drum penetrated through every cell in Taro's body. Slowly beating repeatedly to announce his entrance, it was as if Taro had been transported back to another, ancient life. When the drummer struck the *taiko* for the final time with ritualistic force, the waves of that vibration settled over the room before being pierced by two high-pitched strikes on a bell, *ching-ching,* announcing Taro's entry into the Buddha Hall. All the monks now lowered themselves and sat in *zazen* posture on their cushions, eyes lowered.

When stillness settled into the Buddha Hall, Taro stepped over the threshold with the mouse dangling by its tail from his mouth, turned to the left, and followed a senior monk. Together, in a walking bow, they made their way all around the Hall through the rows.

With the mouse's little body gently swaying, Taro maintained this position of bowed humility as he passed each monk, who bowed back to Taro as was the custom. As he passed by, many thought, *What the hell?* But no one would have known from the disciplined behavior of the monks that they had any judgments or opinions. They maintained their lowered gazes.

After circling past every monk, Taro was directed to walk through the *ryoban*. Now, finally, he was directly in front of *Gennan* Roshi, seated on his high seat.

Roshi leaned in and squinted at Taro. "What's that in your mouth?"

Taro walked a few steps forward, placed the mouse down and said, "It's my gift to you, Roshi." And he picked up the mouse by its tail again and waited.

Roshi said, "I don't see so well. Come a little closer."

With the mouse hanging from his mouth, Taro advanced a few more steps.

Gennan Roshi leaned in, squinted, and said, "Closer."

Taro took a final step and *Gennan* Roshi smacked him mightily with his teaching stick, causing Taro to fall back and release the mouse. Roshi roared, "You don't kill things and bring them into my Buddha Hall!" And at that, Roshi and all the monks broke out in disorderly laughter.

The little gray field mouse, having sufficiently thawed out, was knocked back into consciousness when she slammed into the wall. Flat on her back staring up at the ceiling, she realized her good fortune that no one was paying attention to her. Immediately righting herself, she blasted out of the Buddha Hall, flying towards the safety of the forest.

Taro's head was still spinning from the blow of the teaching stick when *Gennan* Roshi pointed to an empty cushion. "Go now, Taro, and take your seat among the other monks."

Back in the forest, three birds watched over a little gray field mouse with a tuft of white hair leaning to the side on the top of her head. Breathlessly, she shared with a group of animals gathered around her the story of her near-death experience inside the halls of the *Gakiji* Hungry Ghost Zen Buddhist Temple.

The twin buck fawns listened in. Ben leaned toward his brother. "So, you still want to be a Zen student, Ren? Because the fun hasn't even started yet."

CHAPTER *Five*

THE *RYUMONJI* DRAGON GATE ZEN BUDDHIST TEMPLE, located in the southernmost part of the country, had been Ratzitzu's home for the past six months. Coming up through the sewer, he had at first proven to *Ekō* Roshi his capacity to be smart, ambitious, and hard-working. This was the type of student Roshi typically enjoyed. He liked the gritty ones. The ones who didn't come from privilege. The ones who clawed their way up from the bottom. Yes, those types of students were interesting to Roshi, although it took him less than a blink to realize the character flaws that would need to be pounded out of Ratzitzu if he were to continue his training.

The monks who were training with *Ekō* Roshi when Ratzitzu was accepted into the monastery were well aware of his flaws, too. Of course, from their disciplined exteriors, one would never know. But they talked.

None of that was Ratzitzu's concern. *Let Ekō and his stupid band of monks say what they will,* he always thought. All he wanted was to be first. The first animal to make it through Zen training and become a monk. He wanted the bragging rights to prove he was worth something that didn't belong in the sewer. He ached to look different. To be different.

Underground, he was just another sewer rat. Thousands of rats and they all looked the same. But here at *Ryumonji*, he had a chance to be seen, to be original, if he could just hold it together long enough. He could see the headlines of his stunning accomplishment. All the lights and attention would be on him for the world to see. A truly historic event. That's what he craved. And he needed *Ekō* Roshi to get him there.

"I keep wondering why Roshi accepted a rat into *Ryumonji* in the first place. I mean, I know Roshi is forward thinking and all, but a rat? Come on! Such a pompous ass When do you think Roshi's going to do something about Ratzitzu?" one monk whispered to another as the two worked side by side, cleaning the wooden floors.

"No clue. I'm still trying to figure out who could make his clothes, if he ever got that far. How have you found Ratzitzu?"

"My training is hard enough without him. Always elevating himself. He's an arrogant, cocky SOB. . . I would do anything to . . . you know . . ."

"I keep my distance. Otherwise I'm afraid I would wring his neck," the monk said, twisting the towel for emphasis. "It would be so easy."

Although it was believed that rats also brought prosperity to Temples, not too many looked at Ratzitzu in that way. He knew he was the least welcomed novice to enter, but he didn't care. He was used to being looked at with disdain. He had been in training for six months, felt supremely confident for such a nothing period of time, and was never afraid to let the other monks know it. He knew his understanding of Zen wasn't deep at all. *"Buji-zen!"* one monk hissed out of the corner of his mouth in passing, implying his annoyance at Ratzitzu's superficiality and excessive bravado. But Ratzitzu figured his general knowledge of things was good enough to get him through pretty much anything and felt smart enough for whatever came up. More importantly, he was above water level now and no one would be sending him back to the sewer any time soon. Not if he had anything to do with it.

Ekō Roshi, the brilliant, perceptive Zen Master of the *Ryumonji* Dragon Gate Zen Buddhist Temple, often tested his students' understanding against one another publicly. Frequently, a monk's advancement in the ranks was based on the outcome of this public display of performance. Roshi was always pulling the rug out and upsetting expectations in order to train and keep his monks awake and alert.

Over the years, *Ekō* Roshi had found that a monk's being in the spotlight could be a skillful way of poking at sticking points, too, like arrogance, pride, or ego. And, from the beginning, he had certainly been aware of the grumbling and gossiping of his monks about Ratzitzu. Now, after a mere six months, the gossip continued to spread. Roshi knew it was only a matter of time before swift action would need to be taken. But he would let it unfold naturally. He was confident that, one day soon, a teaching moment would present itself. Only then would Roshi see what Ratzitzu was really made of and if he possessed what it took for him to advance in his training at *Ryumonji*.

Commanding his presence from his high seat on the platform one Sunday morning, *Ekō* Roshi violently shook one skinny arm in the air, driving home his point that, "Ninety-nine percent of your suffering is caused because you're asleep!" Punctuating this conclusion, he yelled, "Wake Up!" as he slammed his fist down so hard onto the wooden podium, it shattered, scattering pieces between the aisles and into the laps of the monks seated in the front row of the Dharma Hall.

No one dared move or utter a word.

Aha! The perfect teaching moment had just revealed itself. And *Ekō* Roshi took full advantage of it. Taking his time to scan the large body of monks spread out in neat rows in front of him, he finally shouted, "Ratzitzu! What say you?"

Ratzitzu, ever conscious of his desire to prove what he considered to be his superior understanding, smirked slightly and shot Roshi's challenge back over the bow, saying, "Vast emptiness. No podium."

Roshi's glare hardened. He pointed his finger straight at Ratzitzu's face, "NO! Too conceptual! No pass!"

The public sting shocked Ratzitzu like a slap across the snout. His whiskers began to droop and his body sagged. The eyes of the monks around him started rolling heavenward, and he heard the snickering and throat clearing. Some monks even risked breaking Dharma Hall protocol by ever so quietly whispering to their neighbor.

"So superficial."

"Green and immature."

"He stinks of Zen pride."

Turning his attention away from Ratzitzu, Roshi continued to glare, scanning the faces of his students, finally landing on a novice monk. "Hey! New guy! You over there! What say you?"

The young monk immediately stood up and looked around. Gathering up the scattered pieces of broken podium from the front of the room, he walked out the entryway and deposited the stack of wood in the woodpile outdoors.

Upon the novice's return to his seat in the Dharma Hall, Roshi laughed heartily and clapped his hands, saying, "The new guy wins. Ratzitzu loses."

Ekō Roshi looked over at his attendant, *Kōgen,* as they walked back to Roshi's living quarters later that day. "Do you understand what happened this morning? Why I publicly tested Ratzitzu that way?"

"Yes, Roshi," *Kōgen* said. "You were using skillful means to help Ratzitzu understand his own arrogance."

"Nails that stick up get hammered down. What else? There's more to it."

Kōgen stared straight ahead. His mind had just gone blank.

"Protection!" thundered Roshi, giving his attendant a long, hard, side-glance and a smack on the back of his head. "To protect him from you people. I hear everything!"

Kōgen quickly regained awareness. "Your wisdom and compassion may take a long time for Ratzitzu to acknowledge."

"We'll see. But I think he'll be gone before the evening meal."

It took Ratzitzu about ten days to make his way north. He was carried by the thrust of stinging humiliation and rage. He had heard that some stupid cat had somehow bamboozled the monks into thinking he was worthy and was in training with a *Gennan* Roshi at the *Gakiji* Hungry Ghost Zen Buddhist Temple at the opposite end of the village's forest. This he had to see. Because if it was true, Ratzitzu intended to mercilessly torture the mind of this cat in order to ruin his future. If Ratzitzu could not receive all the glory of being the first animal to become a Zen Buddhist monk, then he would make it his life's work to ruin the chances of any other animal that tried. Whatever it took.

Remi saw it first. The long, naked tail attached to an animal that flattened itself to fit under the foundation of the kitchen. "Hey,

hey, right there!" she hollered as she flapped a wing in the direction of the kitchen. Moving too quickly for the other two to see, she said, "I know what I saw. It's a rat, and it's under the kitchen!"

Rats are diggers and can create extensive, often elaborate, tunnel systems. And Ratzitzu was no exception. His instinctive burrowing nature gave him protection from the eyes of other forest creatures, and this was exactly what he needed right now. He knew he had landed in the right spot on the Temple grounds, because he had been rewarded with a glimpse of a big orange cat sweeping the floor with a broom that was too big for him. *So that's what you look like, you derpy chonk,* Ratzitzu mused as he started digging his way toward a side entrance into the kitchen. Here he would be able to come and go into the kitchen's pantry and steal all the food he needed. *This Gakiji Hungry Ghost Zen Temple is a million times better than Ekō's dump down south,* Ratzitzu thought as he sneered in a smile, showing off his long, yellow teeth.

As Taro swept, his mind wandered. He had seen the birds and had wondered what one of them had gotten all worked up about. They were an excitable bunch, but he appreciated them, as he often saw them looking in the kitchen windows from the branches of the maple trees. Maybe one day the head cook would let him replenish the containers of birdseed located outside the monastery. He would like that. But in the meantime, here he was, still sweeping and washing in the kitchen, although recently the head cook had given him a break by allowing him entry into the pantry to stock and manage items on the lower shelves.

"I told you before, I saw a rat! I'm positive I saw a rat digging under the kitchen. Why would he do that? Everyone here has a proper home in the forest. No one needs to live under the Temple's foundation. Something's wrong," insisted Remi.

"Pipe down already, Remi" Genji said. "If you'd just be quiet, maybe we could figure this out. Stop yelling!"

"Oh, I've got it!" said Hiroto. "We can get Momo to go under the foundation and see what's there. She can report back to us."

"Yes, perfect!" said Remi. "Let's go find her and ask her to help us out."

Momo, the little gray field mouse with the uncontrollable tuft of white on the top of her head, stared at herself in the water at the banks of the creek that ran through the forest. It was impossible to do anything with that hair of hers. It looked like a water fountain squirting in all directions from the top of her head. She was always trying to flatten it or to make it go to one side or the other, but it always sprang back up. It had a mind of its own. And the silly thing wasn't even the same color as the rest of her. Looking at her reflection in the creek's water was disheartening. She wished she had just stayed home.

Suddenly, three birds descended upon her. Forgetting about herself for the moment, she looked up. "Uh, hi. Hi?"

Hiroto bowed in his bird's way. "Hi, Momo. We're here to ask you for your help. For Roshi and Taro."

Immediately, Momo straightened up to full attention, her tuft forgotten. After her near-death experience, she told all the forest creatures that, even though Taro wanted to kill her as an offering to Roshi, he was kind and appreciative in the prayers he had sent up after he had flattened her. She had found this very touching and respected him, not so much for his actions, but for his words at least. "For Roshi? Taro? What can I do?"

Remi said, "I saw a rat digging under the foundation of *Gakiji's* kitchen. I'm sure that's what I saw. We need you to go under the foundation and confirm whether there's anything there or not. Will you do this for us? Because if there is a rat, we need to alert *Gennan* Roshi."

"Of course! I'll do my best," Momo said.

Every creature in the forest loved Roshi and his monks. Because of that, she did not need to consider their request for a second.

The birds chirped happily over one another and finally Hiroto said, "Please get back to us when you have something to report." And with that, the birds bowed again to Momo and flew off.

Momo watched the birds leave. *What have I just done? What if there really is a rat under there? And what if he kills me for real?*

Ratzitzu was completing the tunnel he had burrowed to *Gakiji's* pantry when he heard movement. He stopped and listened with all his senses. Something was coming up behind him. Turning around quickly and bracing himself against the wall, he raised his body to its full height and waited.

Little Momo, head down in concentration, bustled along the freshly dug tunnel when she suddenly bumped into something.

Ratzitzu glared down at her with hard, angry eyes and long, yellow teeth. Looming over her, he blocked any further movement forward.

The sight of this large rat right on top of her shocked Momo so badly, she started to quake. Not even a near-death experience could have prepared her nerves for this. The two stared at each other for a long moment while Momo shook uncontrollably.

Ratzitzu finally broke the stare-down by demanding, "Who are you? What do you want?"

Momo's mouth moved up and down, but no words came out.

Realizing she was no immediate physical threat, Ratzitzu

lowered his front paws to the ground. Surveying the little gray field mouse from top to bottom, he finally said, "What's that mess on top of your head?"

Momo raised her little paws to the mop between her ears. "It's my hair. It's the way I was born," she said, slightly less terrified, being on familiar ground with any conversation having to do with her hair.

Ratzitzu considered this little mouse. She looked like any other field mouse except for all that white hair floss coming out the top of her head. It was odd, but distinctive. She would never be mistaken for one of a thousand other gray field mice. He stood up to his full height again. "I asked you before. What do you want?"

Momo realized how remiss she had been in not being prepared for a confrontation like this and now was caught short. Staring at him, she said, "Oh! Well, nothing. I just saw a hole in the ground and thought I would follow it. You know, just to see where it went."

"Liar!" Ratzitzu roared, thrusting his nose into her face. "You're spying on me! Who sent you? Why are you here?"

Momo jumped back.

"No, no, please!" she said, trying to calm the rat. "I just followed the digging. I'm a mouse. I go into holes, that's all. That's what mice do. You're a good digger. You must have worked very hard to make such a great tunnel."

"Get out! Get out!" Ratzitzu roared. "What I do is of no concern to you. Get out!"

Despite the adrenaline rushing through her body, a part of Momo felt certain Ratzitzu would not kill her. He probably wouldn't even hurt her. All bluster, that one. Standing on her back legs, she stretched to her full height. It wasn't much compared to his, but she looked up. "So, I take it you're new here."

To which Ratzitzu screamed, "GET OUT!"

Aghast, Momo turned and serpentined out of the tunnel back to her own safe home in the forest.

Ratzitzu seethed and beat his fists against his head. He might still be safe, but that mouse had never told him why she had come down his tunnel. She could be his ruin if she talked. He should have demanded an answer before scaring her away. That was a really bad move on his part.

Now, he would need to be especially careful. Even though she seemed harmless, sometimes those types were the worst kind of threat. He hoped he wouldn't have to take her down. But he would if she got in his way. At least he would be able to recognize her with that ridiculous cascade of white hair whipping around her head.

Just thinking about that rat made Momo shake all over again. She feared she had misjudged him. He was so mean and angry. She had not done him any harm. She wondered what he was doing here in the forest under *Gakiji's* foundation. She would tell the birds what she had found. But she would choose her words with care. She didn't want the birds to confront the rat in a way that would cause him to retaliate against her. Momo had to protect her life and her own interests.

And besides, as hard as it was to believe, she found herself thinking there was a little something about him. He was so big. So masculine. So in command. Not hard on the eyes either, if you liked that sort of thing. And she certainly did. Even though he had scared the bejesus out of her, a part of her hoped she had been wrong in her judgment of him.

He seemed scary, but he could still be filled with a lot of smoke and hot air, too. But those teeth. So long and yellow. It was really too much. Everyone had a responsibility to keep themselves groomed. She decided she would leave him some big sticks at the tunnel's entrance to chew on. Some good sticks could file those teeth down and knock that tartar off, too, in no time. Then he would really be a dandy.

After Momo's stomach finally settled down and her heart rate returned to normal, she went off in search of the birds to tell them that, yes, there was a rat under the foundation of *Gakiji*, and that was all she knew. Which was basically true.

CHAPTER *Six*

SIX WEEKS LATER, Taro was released from his regular kitchen duties for the next seven days. This week would mark his first formal training with *Gennan* Roshi in a tradition known as *sesshin*, the essence of Zen.

Taro would follow a rigorous daily schedule along with the other monks. From 4:00 a.m. until 9:00 p.m. it was *zazen*, perform liturgy services, eat breakfast, work practice, *zazen*, liturgy services, eat the midday meal, rest, *zazen*, dharma talk, eat a final small meal. And finally, each monk was granted an opportunity to see Roshi in *dokusan*, a private one-on-one interaction, during that final block of evening *zazen*.

Given the schedule, Taro already felt worn-out and wondered if there were easier ways to enter *dokusan*. It seemed like a lot of work to put in before seeing Roshi at the end of the evening. At this point he felt no gratitude, just exhaustion.

Ratzitzu, however, had already found a solution to this problem. He managed to see Roshi without the long training and practice days. When Ratzitzu heard that Taro was going into this seven-day training period, the rat determined it would be best to find a way to burrow into Roshi's private *dokusan* room so he could hear what the two had to say. Ratzitzu left his hiding place under the pantry and began to scout around the perimeter of the Temple grounds.

Even the first hour of the first day of *sesshin* challenged Taro, who didn't mind sitting and staring at a wall, but he couldn't do it without closing his eyes. And when he closed his eyes, he would start to purr.

First, the monk sitting to his right poked him in the ribs and gave him a stern look. That worked for a few seconds before the purring settled in again. Then the monk to his left flicked him on the ear, and Taro received another nasty scowl. Back and forth. Poke, flick, poke, flick. Finally, Taro had had enough.

He curled up and went to sleep on his cushion. Only then did the purring eventually stop. Many of the monks, who thought Taro was just an exercise of good will on Roshi's part, were willing to overlook this behavior, especially if falling asleep was the worst of it. Some of the monks were grateful they no longer needed to override the purring distraction. A large number were sorry to hear the purring stop, because the rhythmic fluttering helped relax them and deepen their concentration. And there were even some who loved hearing Taro purr because the sound reminded them of home. But no matter what anyone thought, Taro was down for the count the first three morning *zazen* periods on day one. But he woke up in time for breakfast.

Oryoki – Just enough

The formalized practice of *oryoki,* or accepting just enough nourishment into your three nesting bowls each meal, was counterintuitive for Taro. He had always eaten as much as Sachi brought home, because that's how he and his family ate. It's true that a little bit of that edge had been taken off because he was assured of three meals spread out over each day. Still, it wasn't as if they were all-you-could-eat meals. Plus, some of the food was very strange and not so much to his liking.

Taro also missed his mother and Sachi, Nori, and Mika. When he held up the Buddha bowl to offer up prayers of thanks, he chanted with the rest of the monks "*. . . this food is for our teachers, parents, nation, and all Sentient Beings, thus we eat this food with everyone . . .*" and naturally ended up thinking of his family. He always sent a special blessing to them. Meals were a practice and an opportunity to give thanks, just like everything else.

So here Taro found himself this first day in a formal *zendo*, with *Gennan* Roshi staring at him, sometimes making ugly, disapproving faces if Taro dropped his wooden spoon and it clattered to the floor. Or if he ate too noisily or licked the bowl. But Taro was slowly getting the hang of it. It wasn't his intellect. It was more his physical capability and cat nature. After all, paws and hands had some different capabilities.

At the conclusion of the meal, lukewarm water was poured into the Buddha bowl, the biggest of the bowls. This water was used to wash all the remaining bowls and utensils. Since Taro was just learning how to eat *oryoki*-style, he did not realize how efficient the system was. No one had explained anything to him. On that first day, when the lukewarm water was first poured into his bowl, he lapped it up, as any appreciative cat would. After all, those pickles had been so salty.

Suddenly a thunderous voice from the head of the room cut through the sound. "TARO!" Every monk in the *zendo* froze. Taro looked up, a single drop of water falling with a plop from under his chin back into his bowl. He swallowed hard and his whiskers started to twitch as he slowly turned toward Roshi. When Taro's eyes finally locked onto his Master's, Roshi picked up his spatula and, circling it slowly in the water along the sides of his bowl, quietly said, "Like this." Then Roshi ran the spatula around and around the edges, cleaning off the remnants in his bowl.

The relief of the monks in the *zendo,* realizing that nothing more than a shout was going to happen, was so obvious, some of them couldn't help but to start to chuckle out loud as they began to breathe once again. This, of course, started off a wave of laughter as they joyfully ended their morning meal.

Watching from the shadows in a corner of the *zendo,* Ratzitzu witnessed what he considered to be an end-of-meal fiasco. He hated *Gennan* Roshi for showing any kindness to the cat. Ratzitzu fumed as he simmered in his own toxicity. Taro's popularity was starting to take hold, and Ratzitzu was experiencing murderous envy.

Dokusan – Face-to-Face with Roshi

The first day of *sesshin* ended for Taro in anticipation of finally getting to meet *Gennan* Roshi in his private room in a one-on-one encounter known as *dokusan.* Because there were so many students, *Daishin's* call to Roshi's *dokusan* line was precise, "All those facing the West wall in the first row, Roshi's *dokusan* line is open."

Then, out of the stillness in the room, all the monks facing the West wall in the first row immediately leaped up and thundered their way to Roshi's line like a herd of wild animals. It was protocol never to keep Roshi waiting. After all, first come, first served, and there was only a finite amount of time. Some of the monks would get pushed to the side in the stampede, unable to keep up because their feet and legs had gone numb from sitting.

But for Taro, his experience in the marketplace and fear of being trampled drove him forward. He was a spring, ready to uncoil. When he heard Roshi's attendant make the call, he crawled up the monk's backs and shoulders and used their heads to propel himself forward, easily ending up first in line. Unfortunately, the good will many of the monks felt towards

Taro earlier that day was now lost. Cat scratches on a bald head hurt.

Daishin approached Taro and rapped him hard on the head with his knuckle. Leaning into him, he whispered, "Taro, what you just did is not appropriate. You need to move in unison with the other monks. They're not your stepping stones. Stay where you are this time, but if you ever use them that way again, I'll throw you to the back of the line or boot you out completely."

Then *Daishin* told Taro the protocol for properly entering the *dokusan* room. "Here, take this mallet," he said. "Hold it between your paws. When you hear Roshi ring his bell to announce he's ready for the next student in line, strike this *kanshō,* right here. Strike it twice." *Daishin* held up two fingers then touched the specific spot on the bell with one finger.

Continuing in low tones, he said, "Strike, don't clank. It should be a deep, rich *bong* sound you get from a direct, conscious strike. Do it right. Return the mallet here, and then get up quickly, go into the *dokusan* room and close the door. Do a full bow in front of Roshi. Make sure your head touches the ground. He'll tell you what to do after that. In the meantime, sit here and be still. Stop swishing your tail." Then *Daishin* was gone.

Taro looked at the *kanshō* in front of him. It was a magnificent bell, about eight inches long, cast from bronze, and hanging from a polished wooden frame about six inches off the ground.

The ringing of the bells back and forth was an ancient communication that had been passed down through the lineage. It meant that Roshi was ready to receive the student and, in turn, the student announced awareness of the invitation. A profound, wordless interaction. A timeless song.

But the *kanshō* intimidated Taro, and the handle of the mallet was long for him, which was also worrisome. He ran the instructions through his head, praying for the presence of mind to strike and not clank.

Ding-a-ling-a-ling. Ding-a-ling-a-ling. Roshi's bell summoned the next student in line. Taro jumped up. Now, he was too tall and stood above the bell's sweet spot. Clank!

The sound ripped through the air and sent shockwaves through the monks sitting behind him. Some winced, but most gritted their teeth as they attempted to stabilize the racing of their hearts with deeper breathing.

Taro frantically commanded his thoughts. *Breathe! Slow down, slow down. Do it again.* Bonk! There was nothing more he could do. He apologized mentally to the monks in line as he quickly returned the mallet, made his way to the door, and pushed it open.

Taro entered the *dokusan* room and completed a full bow in front of *Gennan* Roshi, mindful to touch his head to the ground. Roshi looked at him, smiled, and said, "Welcome. Please sit down," as he motioned to the cushion in front of him. For an average-sized person, the monk would have been practically knee to knee with Roshi.

Gennan Roshi said, "Come to the edge of the mat. All the way up to the edge. Come closer."

Taro had heard those words before, and he felt they did not bode well for him.

The small room was lit only by a candle flickering to the right of a large, bronze Buddha statue placed on top of a rectangular black walnut altar. A stick of incense burned in a bowl placed directly in front of the statue. The top quarter of the incense had already turned to ash and fallen into the packed powder that held it upright. To the left of the statue sat a short vase with fragrant pine cuttings and a few red berries. The room was completely still.

Glancing quickly past the altar, Taro saw a scroll of a circle on one wall. He would later learn this *ensō*, the round, incomplete circular form, represented the full, bright moon of Buddha's enlightenment.

But most importantly, Taro's attention was riveted on *Gennan* Roshi, who sat in front of him in the semi-darkened room.

Roshi's robes were tucked under his crossed legs, the black georgette fabric outlining his entire body perfectly. In front of Roshi on his cushion was his folded bowing mat. Lying across his lap, Roshi balanced his teaching stick, the same stick that he had used to smack Taro the first time they met.

Taro looked at that stick, already in Roshi's hand, and wondered what was going to happen next. His mouth went dry.

Roshi looked steadily at Taro and quietly addressed him. "So, tell me, Taro. What brings a cat to *Gakiji*?"

And in the moment of that question, so simple and unencumbered, yet vast and unfeigned, Taro forgot about the stick. His heart broke open, and a feeling of love for *Gennan* Roshi began to arise within him.

"I want to know my place in this world. I want to find my purpose in life."

Gennan Roshi breathed in deeply, exhaling slowly. His *dokusan* room was small but infinite, stretching beyond all knowledge and imagination. Accepting everything, eliminating nothing. Here, the Milky Way existed equally alongside the animal dung in the snow. Roshi reflected on the many students who had come before Taro and had done the hard work in this room. The ones who kept their feet to the fire, when quitting would have been so much easier. He wondered if Taro had what it took.

"Where are you now?" Roshi asked.

Taro didn't know how to respond. "Well, um, here, I guess. But I meant, you know, I'm talking about my place out there in the world," he said, raising his paw. "My father and only brother were killed by a horse last spring. I feel there has to be more than just becoming my father. I mean, that's important for our family, I know, but I can't be my father. I don't want to be him. As a first-born, I was never good at providing, and knew I was letting everyone down," he said, his eyes downcast.

"Who is in your family?"

"Well, my mother, of course, and I have three sisters. Sachi, Nori and Mika."

Roshi considered Taro. "Who is taking care of your family, now that you are no longer with them?"

Taro sat up straighter and said, "My sister Sachi. She's the best provider in the whole world. She always finds meat and good food."

"I see. And your other two sisters? What roles do they play in the family?"

"Mama and Nori take care of Mika. She can't live on her own. She will always need full time care. We don't know what's wrong with her. It's just the way she is," Taro said.

Roshi closed his eyes after that for so long, Taro thought he might have fallen asleep.

But Roshi wasn't asleep. He was very much awake. Sometimes the dim lighting in the room with the dancing shadows from the candlelight tired his eyes, but it was nothing more than that.

Finally, he opened his eyes. "And your mother? How is she?"

Ah! Taro's mother. He could still hear her angry spits and hisses. He, too, wondered how she was doing. All he knew was he was sending her prayers to forgive him and blessings every day for a good and healthy life. "I don't know. She was so angry when I left," Taro said.

Gennan Roshi thought for several more moments, this time with his eyes open. He finally said, "Are you really sure you want to know your place in this world?"

Taro responded quickly, "Yes, Roshi! Yes, I do!"

Gennan Roshi said evenly, "We'll see." And with that, he reached over, picked up his hand bell, and Taro was *ding-a-ling-a-linged* out of the room.

Startled, Taro immediately blurted, "But Roshi! What about my place in this world?"

To which *Gennan* Roshi just nodded and smiled with the bell in his hand. *Ding-a-ling-a-ling.*

Ratzitzu considered the conversation he had just heard. *So Taro was a loser,* but Ratzitzu figured as much. *Taro had lost his father and brother in some kind of accident, and then left his family and a sister who couldn't live on her own. What was her name? Nika? Moki? Whatever. No one cared. And then Taro admitted his mother blew a gasket when he left but had no idea what was going on with her now. Boo hoo. The dummy was basically asking Gennan to tell him what to do next. Hey, blockhead! Why don't you go figure it out yourself like everyone else has to?*

Unfortunately for Ratzitzu, he completely missed the essence of Roshi's revelation.

The next morning during work practice, when all the monks busily engaged in their assigned duties of cooking and cleaning the Temple, *Gennan* Roshi left through the main gate, carrying extra birdseed and some powdered incense wrapped up like a small package. It was the head cook's responsibility to weigh and measure the seed so there would be enough food to supplement the birds and small creatures through the winter.

Roshi knew that, but today he didn't care, making a mental note to hopefully remember to tell the head cook what he had done. He needed a gift of appreciation to extend to those three birds who spent time peering in the kitchen window. They had shown a curiosity and interest in Taro, and now Roshi had a job for them.

Gennan Roshi made his way to an assemblage of cherry trees on the top of a rolling hill where several small wooden buckets, now half emptied of bird seed, hung from a few of the lower branches. He scanned the sky, then sat down in *zazen* under one of the trees and waited.

Before long, two cardinals and a red-winged blackbird

lighted on a low branch within easy reach of where Roshi sat. *Gennan* Roshi opened his eyes and smiled. "Thank you for coming," he said. "I have a job of personal interest and hope you can make a trip for me."

The three birds expressed their eagerness to help by flapping their wings and bowing as birds do. They would do anything *Gennan* Roshi asked of them. After all, he and his monks helped to sustain them during the cold winter months.

Hiroto said, "Roshi, we are at your service."

Gennan Roshi smiled. "Hiroto, Remi, and Genji. I would like you to find Taro's family and observe them. I am especially interested in how his mother is doing." He fumbled in his long sleeves, finally pulling out a piece of paper and unfolding it. He looked at the paper for a moment and then deciphered the information for them. "This is the location Taro gave us when he first entered *Gakiji*. I think it's close to the marketplace, which is in the center of the village."

The birds looked back and forth at one another, then shrugged, "We're not sure what you mean, because we've never been to the marketplace, but we will figure it out," said Remi.

Roshi continued, "I think it might be easier if you find his sister Sachi in the marketplace and follow her home. I understand she's quite an accomplished provider. Long dark gray fur, bright green eyes."

Hiroto nodded. "It will probably be easier for us to find Sachi. We'll start in the market."

As *Gennan* Roshi stood, the birds made ready for flight. "Wait!" he cried out. "Two more things. First, you need nourishment for the trip." Roshi emptied the seed he had carried from the kitchen into one of the buckets. "And Hiroto, I would like you to take this powdered incense and lay it in a place where Taro's mother will find it. It's just a small pouch. I made sure the package would not be too heavy for you, and there's a loop for carrying. But it will have enough scent for his mother to be reminded of Taro. I am hoping she will receive it as a gift from him. And remember, you're just observing. No interaction yet."

Gennan Roshi placed the small package bound in string on a low cherry tree branch. Then he waved to the birds. "I look forward to your safe return."

Taro was once again in the kitchen as part of his daily work duty during *sesshin*. The head cook had him moving goods in and out of the pantry, stocking, and bringing food and ingredients to the cooks. Back and forth to the kitchen, up and down the shelves, in and out of the pantry. For Taro, who had always considered himself to be a bottom dweller, work practice was turning into a vertical workout. He had to be very careful not to get underfoot for fear of being crushed. A leftover dread from his days of scavenging in the marketplace. But at least he was useful here. He provided a service.

Once when he crossed in front of a monk and was almost accidently kicked in the ribs, he remembered what *Daishin* had told him in the *dokusan* line. *You need to move in unison with the rest of the monks.* Taro remembered the first time he had seen the monks outside the Temple gate on New Year's Day, sweeping and raking, working and moving as one body. Just as water flows around and not through the rocks. Taro appreciated how important it would be for him to find his place within the living masterpiece of life in the monastery.

Kōan – The direct pointing to reality.

Taro felt more centered by the evening of the second full day of *sesshin*. He eagerly awaited his opportunity to see Roshi once again.

When the *dokusan* line was called on his side of the *zendo*,

Taro left his cushion quickly, but not so quickly as to be reprimanded again by *Daishin*. He ended up fourth in line. That wasn't so bad. When his time came, Taro was ready with the mallet and struck the *kanshō* properly when Roshi rang his hand bell.

The glow thrown off by the flickering candle and the smell of incense that dominated the *dokusan* room made Taro feel he was in a safe, sacred space. *Gennan* Roshi motioned him to the cushion, and Taro once again approached and sat down. They gazed at one another for a moment. But Taro was worried that Roshi would *ding-a-ling-a-ling* him out of the room before he even got started, so Taro began right away.

"Roshi, please help me understand my place in this world. Not my father's place, or my birth order place, but *my* place. I feel my life so far has not been my own."

Gennan Roshi considered Taro and then said, "If you want to reach an enlightened state of awareness on this, I want you to study *kōans*. If you want to work with me, these *kōans* are how you will get there."

"Who are the Cohens, Roshi?" Taro asked.

Gennan Roshi chuckled. "Taro, the Cohens can't help you. I said *kōans*. You can think of a *kōan* as a statement or even a story that you can't understand with your logical mind but that creates the territory which allows you access to something much greater. This is where you will begin to find what you are looking for."

"Oh. So it will help me find out who I am and where my place is in this world?"

Roshi's gaze was level. "If you want to find out who you are in this world, show me your original face before your father was born."

Taro's mouth fell open. "What? What does that have to do with my father? I'm asking about me!" Taro immediately regretted the edge in his voice as *Gennan* Roshi picked up his teaching stick from across his lap and put one end on the ground, balancing his forearm on the opposite end. Moving his face closer to Taro's, Roshi said, "When you can clearly present your understanding of this *kōan* to me, you will begin to see who you are and what your place is in this world."

"But I don't know how to do that." Taro's voice trembled as he kept an eye on the stick.

"Sit in the inquiry with your whole body and mind, as if you had a fire upon your head. Eventually you'll feel like a mosquito attacking an iron bowl. Your inquiry will feel futile. But if you persist, you will come to understand."

Gennan Roshi saw the doubt building in Taro's eyes, and he could feel his hesitancy. "This is not for everyone. You will come up against all your lies, your nonsense, all the manipulations you've used to get people to like you and give you things. You'll come up against your phony cat act, too. All of it. But if you really want to know your place as badly as you say, follow my instructions and do what I tell you to do."

Taro stared at Roshi, eyes starting to water. His whiskers twitched. "My phony cat act?"

"Yes. Just sit in the inquiry as if your life depended on it. If you want the freedom and awareness you say you seek, you're going to have to work for it."

"So," Roshi continued, raising his teaching stick and pointing it directly at Taro. "Quickly! Show me your original face before your father was born!"

Taro's mind scattered in chaos. He was transfixed by the stick pointing at his face.

Roshi understood this. All his students started out this way. As a note of encouragement to Taro, Roshi leaned back and lowered his teaching stick onto his lap. "You've been blessed to get this far. Don't quit. Keep going. You can do it. Put yourself into it. Not everyone answers the call, but you might." *Ding-a-ling-a-ling.*

Ratzitzu, watching from the sidelines of Roshi's *dokusan* room, slapped his paw to his forehead and felt a headache coming on. *Not kōan study! This will take forever with someone as clueless as Taro. What an ass!*

Ratzitzu didn't expect to be rewarded with high insight or for Taro to spout brilliant understanding. *My God, not by a long shot. But it will be fun to watch him fail.* It's not as if Ratzitzu had had any experience with this *kōan*. He hadn't and was himself, clueless. He would not have been able to express the spirit of this *kōan* if it had punched him between the eyes. But Ratzitzu enjoyed his front row seat in the *dokusan* room. And the nuts and fruit he had taken from the pantry tasted pretty good, too, even though he was dropping a few more fresh ones than usual. Must have been all that fruit.

The three birds, bellies full of birdseed, playfully chased one another as they exited the forest, Hiroto in the lead, carrying the bag of powdered incense. They periodically rested on branches and shrubs, as the cardinal's short, round wings were not built for long distance flying. And Hiroto wasn't used to carrying things very far in his beak. But they had an important job to do and did not want to disappoint Roshi. As they approached the outskirts of the village, they slowed down and became more serious and focused.

The marketplace in the center of the village was designed around a central area of cobblestone streets, and the breakfast crowd lingered at outdoor tables. The lucky ones were closest to the open fire pit in the center. Those sitting farther away held onto large cups filled with coffee or hot chocolate to keep their hands warm. It was a clear, crisp day, and the fruit and vegetable stands were stocked and open. The birds, balanced atop the pitched roof of a bakery shop, had an ideal view of the marketplace.

People talked and laughed. Despite being bundled up against the cold, the children played. Balloons bobbed in the air, connected by colorful ribbons to little wrists, hands covered by mittens. The pleasant scene was abruptly disrupted by shouting and cursing coming from one of the stalls at the far end of the marketplace.

The three birds' heads turned. A vendor yelled and shook his arms. Spit flew out of his mouth. He had an onion in his hand that he appeared ready to launch. But the thief had moved too swiftly, and the man had no choice but to return the onion to its bin and punctuate the air with a few final curses.

The birds scanned the area for the offender. They finally saw him several hundred feet away underneath a vacant table, calmly licking his paw and wiping his face. His short black hair and yellow eyes were a dead giveaway that this was not Sachi. The birds sighed. That would have been too easy. After watching the comings and goings of the crowd for a while with no luck, they thought they might be better off spreading out.

The birds agreed to start by covering three different places. Since lugging the incense from the forest had tired him, Hiroto would stay in the marketplace on the bakery's roof.

Genji flew to the right and found he was in a neighborhood within moderate walking distance to the marketplace. If he perched on the spire of a small church located at the end of the block, he had a good view of the area.

Remi turned to the left and wound up in a commercial section of town. She thought it very possible that Taro's family would be located somewhere near here, and she hoped to bring back a positive report. She settled atop the rooster's head of a dry goods store's weathervane and felt she was in a very good position.

The birds sang back and forth periodically to keep in touch and agreed to add a trill at the end if they spotted something they thought would lead them to Sachi or if they needed help. Later, they would reconvene on the bakery shop roof.

The morning was winding down without much action. From the rooftop of the bakery shop, Hiroto was entertained by the people and animals moving around, but Sachi had not shown herself.

Genji, in the residential area of town, was bored. He found himself flying from one section of the neighborhood to another, just to stay alert. Nothing had shown up for him but kids and dogs.

Remi, in the commercial section, felt she had more at stake because she still believed Sachi and her family lived somewhere in this area. She stayed observant, staring down while scanning as many streets as she could from the top of the rooster's head.

The furry gray cat peered around the corner of a brick building before darting across the street. Atop the weathervane, Remi's heart started to beat excitedly as she went on full alert. She wanted to alert the others but decided to first watch the gray cat as it slowly strolled down the sidewalk, brushing up against the sides of the buildings as it went by. One block more, and the cat turned away from the direction of the marketplace, quickly ran across the street again, and bounded up a short set of steps outside a fabric store. It sat down, faced the door, and started to *meow*.

Remi flew in for a closer look. A few minutes later, she saw an old woman come outside to the stoop and gather up the cat. Cradling her cat as they went inside, she shook her finger in his face and lovingly scolded him for crossing the street. Remi didn't remember anything being said about Taro's family living with an old woman. This must be a dead end. Good thing she kept her trill to herself.

As the sun was leaving the high noon position, all three birds needed a break. They reunited on the roof of the bakery shop, and then flew down to the ground and pecked at breadcrumbs that had been brushed off the tablecloths.

Suddenly the birds heard a loud commotion coming from the left. A water glass had crashed onto the cobblestone street. A man, half-standing over the table, shouted, "Hey! What are you doing? Get out of here! Get out!"

The trio instantly flew up onto the back of an empty chair to watch the show from this low vantage point.

A long-haired, dark gray cat had pushed off the table, knocked a glass of water onto the ground and sped off. It stopped, turned around, and sat on its haunches. The bright green eyes were unblinking as it looked back at the man who was still shouting. Two long curly fries were sticking out each side of the cat's mouth.

Of course, Sachi had no idea the three birds were interested in her as she ate the fries to taunt the man. There was never a lack of good food in the marketplace. She would get something more nutritious for the family later. For now, it was just great fun eating the fries in front of the man, who was still so upset that they had been taken from him.

The three birds looked at one another, and Genji whistled. This had to be Sachi.

For the remainder of the afternoon, they watched as she anticipated, calculated, leapt, and scored. Sometimes, the diners had no idea that they had just lost a portion of their meal. Except for that one clumsy move where she had knocked over a glass of water, she was smooth and graceful. The birds were impressed.

Remi turned to her companions. "Here's what I think we're supposed to do. We follow Sachi home, watch what happens with her mother. Hiroto deposits the incense on a windowsill or someplace where the mother will find it, and then we go home."

"No," Genji countered. "I think we should wait until Sachi leaves the marketplace and then we should talk to her. Find out how her mother is and what's been going on since Taro left. Play it low keyed and thoughtful. Concerned."

"That's too risky," interjected Hiroto. "She won't know us and may think we're spying on her, or that maybe we're gathering information to do something bad to her family or Taro."

"We *are* spying on her. But we're birds. How threatening can we be to a cat?" Genji whistled loudly.

"Stop! Roshi said to just observe," Remi said.

"She might eat us!" Hiroto protested.

Around and around and around this went until the three birds were hooting and tooting so loudly at one another, they began to draw attention to themselves. Sachi looked up. When she saw the three birds on the back of the chair, her tail began to swish as she crouched down into pounce position.

"Uh, oh. There! You see? Now you've gone and done it," Remi hollered.

"Me?" Genji screeched.

"Be quiet, you two! On my count of three, we're flying back to the roof of the bakery shop. One! Two! Three! Come on, come on! Hurry, hurry, she's gonna spring!" Hiroto shrieked.

Sachi watched as the three birds took off. Too bad. They would have been fun to chase. But she wasn't interested in cardinal or red-wing blackbird for dinner. She liked her meals already cooked. Anyway, time to go. She didn't like to make her mother worry. Gathering up her loot in a burlap cloth, she picked it up in her mouth, and trotted off towards home.

"Come on, let's go. She's on the move," Remi said to the group.

Following Sachi, the colorful birds stayed back so they would be as inconspicuous as possible.

Sachi hurried away from the marketplace, headed towards the commercial section of town, then veered off through a mixed neighborhood of shops and homes. She made her way to an area towards the outskirts of town, where it was more country-like and open. Quickly moving down a dirt driveway, she turned to the side of the main house and darted through an opening into a large crawlspace. Her family waited for her under the house.

"Sachi," her mother said, relieved. "Thank goodness you're home. We were starting to worry."

Sachi looked around at her family. She loved them and didn't like to upset them. "Here, look what I've brought for us. Lots of meat and some bread. Nori, I found a slice of salmon especially for you."

Nori purred loudly and licked her sister's face.

The crawlspace the family lived in was an excellent home. Even better, they had access to the entire farmhouse whenever they wanted. There was more than enough room and each had areas they could retreat to, even though they usually preferred staying close together.

A line of Cinnamon Barberry shrubs paralleled the side of the farmhouse. Luckily for the cardinals, they could hide within the dark orange shrubs and continue their surveillance undetected. Hiroto stood out a little, but he would manage.

The birds watched as the cat family ate their meal. When all the food had been eaten, Sachi went off to a far corner, curled up, and went to sleep. Nori took Mika to an opposite corner where she could play with whatever caught her interest until she fell asleep. Then Nori covered her sister with her own body to keep her safe until it was time to wake up again.

Reiko watched her babies with pride and gratitude. She was astonished that Sachi had picked up the skill of finding food so quickly from Taro. He must have been an excellent teacher. But oh. Taro. She missed him so. Her anger had faded, replaced now with a deep regret that she had not tried to understand him. Appreciate him more fully. At least give him a chance. She longed to see him again. If for no other reason than to know he was healthy and well.

She often felt haunted by her unkind words and the way she'd acted when he brought her those beautiful buttons. He had only been trying to please her. Letting out a soft, low guttural sound, she walked to a corner in their crawlspace where she had placed a box she had found when the family first moved in.

On top of the box was a gray velvet pouch. Reiko took it down and opened it. Out poured eight shiny black buttons studded with rhinestones. She picked one of them up. Holding it in front of her face, she licked it several times before cradling it to her chest. She lay down surrounded by the buttons and closed her eyes.

Hiroto whispered, "I think she misses him. This is a good time to drop the incense at the opening to their home. Maybe she will come and get it." Using his beak to gather the small pouch he had laid in the shrub, he quickly flew to the access opening, where he dropped the gift. In a flash, he rejoined the others in the shrubbery.

Reiko smelled it before she even opened her eyes. Taro! She lifted her head up and looked around the room. All she saw were three furry lumps, breathing rhythmically. Then she saw something in the middle of the entrance and jumped up to see what it was. A few buttons rolled off her. As she approached, the essence of Taro became stronger and stronger. And when she opened the bag of powdered incense, she was drawn back to the first time she had smelled this scent on him. The Temple in the forest.

Holding the bag in both paws, she closed her eyes and placed it to her face, breathing in deeply. This scent was everything Reiko knew Taro wanted. On the next inhalation of the incense, she realized in her mother's heart that Taro was fine and was living the life he longed to live. And in that moment, she was overcome with joy for her son.

CHAPTER *Seven*

GENNAN ROSHI YAWNED, rubbed his eyes, and leaned forward in a long, slow stretch. Righting himself, he assumed a perfect *zazen* posture, his left hand cradling his right. His thumbs touched in a natural arch above the palms so lightly that a piece of rice paper could easily slide up and down between them. He took a deep breath and exhaled.

Gennan Roshi knew. There was a rat in the corner of his *dokusan* room. Momo knew, the birds knew, and now he knew, too. But it wasn't just any rat. It was the rat from *Ekō* Roshi's Temple. The rat that couldn't perform under pressure and left *Ryumonji* at the end of *Ekō's* now famous dharma talk. Word had gotten out fast. *Ekō* Roshi informed all the Zen masters in charge of Temples in the area to be on the alert. The rat was not to be trusted.

When *Gennan* Roshi was first told by the monk who cleaned his *dokusan* room of the pilings of rat dung, fruit peels, and seed husks in the corner, Roshi initially thought to expose the rat and banish him publicly. It would have been an easy action to take, and then he would have been done with the rat. But Roshi rarely acted on his first impulse. After he let his mind settle down, he chose what he believed would be a more skillful solution. For starters, he told the monk who cleaned his room to sweep up all the turds but to leave some of the peelings and husks behind in the corner. He wanted the rat to feel comfortable and familiar in the corner.

Then Roshi turned his thoughts to Taro. He was growing fond of the big ginger cat. And now it was time to begin applying some pressure to determine the cat's flexibility, stamina, and worthiness of the privilege of being ordained as a Zen Buddhist monk someday. But first things first. He would see what Taro did with the original face *kōan*. *Gennan* Roshi loved the ancient wisdom of *kōans* and their modern-day applications. The rigor it required to work in earnest with them was unbearable sometimes, but worth it once realization was achieved.

Gennan Roshi yawned again, thinking of all the original faces that had come before Taro. He picked up his bell. *Ding-a-ling-a-ling.*

Taro could not have been more miserable. He was trying his best, but the idea of an original face before his father was born was beyond his understanding. *How was that even possible and why did it matter?* He didn't understand how thinking about faces would help him with his life's purpose.

When *Daishin* called the *dokusan* line on Taro's side of the *zendo,* Taro found himself not moving as quickly as he had before. Being farther back in the line was fine with him. It gave more time between him and the dreaded, inevitable face to face with Roshi. But eventually Taro rang the *kanshō* in reply to Roshi's bell. Taro's heart started beating faster as he made his way into *dokusan*.

"So, how do you understand this original face? Show me!" said Roshi once Taro had sat down.

Taro hesitated.

"Too late!" said Roshi.

"But I don't know what to do," Taro whined.

"Forget about yourself! Stop thinking! Get out!" *Ding-a-ling-a-ling.*

Making his way back to his seat in the *zendo,* Taro felt frustrated, but it was his first attempt, after all. He figured Roshi would give him a break and help him out. Taro vowed that he would do everything perfectly so Roshi would take pity on him and give him the answer. But in the meantime, Taro would have to figure out how he was going to do that.

The intensity of *sesshin* was heating up, and Roshi saw students more frequently. The next call to the *dokusan* line, Taro was ready with a response and quickly found his way close to the front of the line. On cue, he rang the *kanhsō* and entered the room.

Face to face once again, Roshi asked the same question, "How do you see this original face? Show me the spirit of this *kōan.*"

Taro looked at Roshi and scrunched up his face, tongue hanging out as if he had no teeth, shaking a palsied paw back and forth.

Roshi looked at him expressionlessly, which was not easy because the presentation was so ridiculous. "That's nonsense! This isn't a guessing game. Stop thinking about it. Get out of here!" *Ding-a-ling-a-ling.*

Ratzitzu was enjoying the show. *Two down. Let's go for three, or four, or more! Come on, dough boy. You are such a boob. You don't have a clue. You'll never make it, so I'm pretty sure I can relax and stop worrying. It's only a matter of time.*

Taro was starting to feel a prickly sense of apprehension. This last *dokusan* did not go well. He knew he would not be able to out-smart Roshi. What did *stop thinking about it* mean, anyway? He'd have to think about that some more.

The next time the *dokusan* line was called on Taro's side, he stayed seated. *Daishin* came up behind him and fiercely whispered, "What are you doing? Get up! Get in line!"

Taro shook his head. No. Nothing had shifted, nothing had changed for him. He had no idea what to do and no answer to the *kōan*.

Daishin picked him up and put him in the front of the line, saying, "You're next."

Face to face once again, Roshi said, "This original face. Show it to me quickly!"

"Uh . . . uhhh," Taro stammered.

Roshi shook his head. "Drop off all thoughts and stop thinking! Let go of everything. Your concepts and ideas. Let go! You'll get it. Don't quit. Now get out of here!" *Ding-a-ling-a-ling.*

Leaving the *dokusan* room, *Daishin* goaded him, "Well, did you get it?"

Shaking his head, Taro said, "No."

"Then get back in there!" *Daishin* said, picking Taro up again and pushing him through the door, much to the annoyance of the monk who was already on the threshold, ready to enter the room.

Roshi looked at Taro and said, "Why are you here again? I can tell you don't have it. Get out!" *Ding-a-ling-a-ling.*

"Well?" asked *Daishin* with a stern look on his face.

Taro shook his head *no* once again. He was embarrassed and self-conscious. Several of the monks in line had actually opened their eyes and glared at him. Taro got the message.

Daishin, exasperated, pointed in the direction of the *zendo* and whispered harshly, "Just go back to your seat. Go! Go sit!"

Ratzitzu, of course, was delighted with Taro's failures. Any time Taro failed felt like a win for Ratzitzu. And he was planning on taking as many wins to the bank as possible. *Hallelujah!* He rubbed his paws together, did a little dance, and pooped again in the corner.

Now great doubt was rising up in Taro as he sat in *zazen*.

If I go forward, it's wrong. If I go back, it's wrong, so I can't do either. So what am I supposed to do? Taro asked himself over and over. He couldn't see to the other side of this *kōan*, if there even was an *other* side. *Maybe it was all a big con. But other monks had successfully worked with kōans. So there had to be something there.*

Taro was stuck in a loop. He didn't know the answer. And he was sure he would never find his life's purpose this way. And the more he thought, the more squeezed he felt. The more squeezed he felt, the more he remembered to try to relax and stop thinking, but that only led to more thinking about not thinking.

Taro's head began to pound and his doubt and frustration rose up like a wave inside of him and he banged his paws to his head. Again and again, he silently demanded of himself, *Come on, come on!! Think! Wait. I mean, don't think. Stop. Stop thinking.* But, when no glimmer of an opening presented itself, his thoughts turned hard and bitter against himself. *I can't do this. I'm not smart enough. I'm not special. Cats can't do this. It's not meant for me. I can't do this. I can't. I can't.* Over and over, and when enough pressure had built up, an enormous cry erupted from within Taro that shattered the still minds of all the seated monks in the *zendo*. The monitor on Taro's side of the room, responsible for keeping tranquility in the space, yelled out, "Quiet!"

Many of the monks present that day would later tell the story of how a screeching cat in the *zendo* took them out of their conceptual minds and brought them to enlightenment.

Unfortunately, that was not what happened to Taro.

Taro forced himself to inquire into this original face, but he kept drifting into thoughts of his father. He was still angry that his father had died. Everything had shifted at that point, including his mother's expectations. He felt incompetent in his home. Yet being in the monastery, he also felt incompetent as well as guilty for leaving his family. And here was Roshi, holding up his father's face to him. And all Taro could do was think that he'd better hurry up and find his life's purpose.

Roshi had told him to drop off all concepts, thoughts, and ideas. Taro wondered how he was supposed to do that. He didn't even really know what that meant. *Maybe the face isn't original at all, or maybe this face was created after my father was born, not before. So when would that have been?* Just thinking about his father's face sent Taro into a downward spiral. *But maybe the kōan is really about someone else's face. Or maybe it isn't even about a face at all. That would be Zen, wouldn't it? But then what? And how am I supposed to stop thinking but still think at the same time? Wait. What?* Taro felt his head would explode.

Another call to the *dokusan* line. Taro dug his claws in and continued to sit.

Once again, *Daishin* came up behind Taro and poked him in the side. "Get up! Roshi wants to see you."

Taro, firmly grounded on his cushion, vigorously shook his head. "No! I don't want to see him!"

Daishin said, "Suit yourself. This isn't for everyone."

Taro turned his head slightly towards *Daishin,* then back towards the wall. "I'm not quitting!" Taro said.

Daishin regarded him and moved on.

The final call to *dokusan* for the day was in the 7:00 p.m. block of *zazen*. Taro stayed seated when his side of the *zendo* was called. *Daishin* came up behind him, poked him again in the ribs, and hissed, "Get up. Now! You're next." Taro heaved a sigh and started to walk slowly to the line.

Daishin finally had had enough, picked him up and deposited

Taro in front of the *dokusan* door. "Get in there and bow toward Roshi as if you had some respect and appreciation for this training."

Once in the *dokusan* room, Taro bowed deeply to Roshi. He had no idea what to do next except sit down in front of his teacher. Roshi leaned in towards Taro and again asked, "What is this original face before your father's face was created, Taro? Show it to me. Show me quickly!"

Taro panicked, and he started making googly eyes at Roshi. *Idiot!* The minute Taro did that he felt so stupid, that he quickly covered his eyes, as if to erase what he had just done.

Gennan Roshi looked at Taro with his paws covering his crazy-making eyes. Unbeknownst to Taro, Roshi smiled. This ginger cat who had insisted on entrance into *Gakiji* to train along with the rest of the students, who had chosen to stay here, to do the hard work of becoming a monk, was doing just fine. He was right where he was supposed to be at this point in his training. Roshi had noticed a subtle shift in Taro's demeanor when he first came in and bowed. Taro was at the outer edges of understanding the essence of the *kōan*. Roshi leaned in on him and said evenly, "Come back when you have something!" *Ding-a-ling-a-ling.*

Taro was beside himself. He felt so stupid. And that bell. That bell! What he wouldn't give to hit Roshi over the head with it. All he had hoped for was that Roshi would help him out just a little. But, no. That bell was the final straw! Before Taro bolted out of the *dokusan* room, he turned his body, raised his tail and flicked it in an impolite manner at Roshi. *Enough with the stupid kōan! That's it. I'll figure out something else to do* he thought as he bolted through the Temple gate and headed into the forest.

Ratzitzu saw the entire thing. *Oh. My. God! This is beyond fantastic. And that disgusting tail thing at the end? Absolute perfection.* Ratzitzu started to cheer. No! The cheering could wait. He had one more thing to do first to ensure that Taro would leave *Gakiji* forever. Pivoting on one foot, Ratzitzu banked a few more turds before he exited the *dokusan* room. Making his way around the complex, he ran out into the forest in search of Taro.

When Taro finally stopped running, he was exhausted. He could not outrun what he despised about himself. His disgrace was right there in front of him, no matter where he was or how far he went. He carried it with him as his own common denominator. Wherever he went, there he was.

The best Taro could do was to roll himself up under the protection of a cherry tree. He believed he would never do anything worthwhile. It was better to just make himself as small as he could to protect what little dignity he had left. Taro wasn't going to make the cut in Zen training at *Gakiji*. By reacting so badly and running away, he had lost his chance to understand his true purpose in life. *Gennan* Roshi would never want to work with him again. And oh, that rude gesture with his tail! *What was I thinking?* Taro curled up as tightly as he could, paws over his head. Who did he think he was? He wasn't even worthy of having a purpose.

Taro heard a rustling sound and sat up. A large, black rat stared at him with bright, shiny eyes. Taro sensed a hostile, unpleasant attitude coming from him. The rat approached Taro and stood a little too close. Taro backed up. "Who are you?" he demanded with false bravado.

"I'm here to help you," Ratzitzu said in a silky voice. "My name is Ratzitzu, and I am at your service. *Gennan* personally asked me to escort you safely out of the forest."

There was something about the way the rat was speaking that triggered suspicion in Taro. He had learned early on that no one would ever refer to Roshi as just *Gennan*. It was rude and disrespectful to address a Zen Master by his dharma name alone. "I don't believe you!" Taro cried.

"I've been watching you, Taro," Ratitzu continued in a voice still soft and smooth. "I've seen everything you've done. I understand what *Gennan* means when he tells me you're not the one. Come on. We'll walk together to the edge of the forest. Then you can go home," Ratzitzu said, clenching his jaw to keep from screaming.

"You're lying to me. Roshi never told you to do anything!" Taro said as he dug his claws into the ground.

"No, you're wrong. *Gennan* only wants me to help you leave the forest safely tonight," Ratzitzu said, gritting his teeth. He could barely breathe.

"I'm not going anywhere with you!"

"Come on, let's go, Taro."

"No! I won't!"

That was the final straw. Standing up on his hind legs, Ratzitzu exposed long, yellow teeth. Unable to hold himself back any longer, he erupted in a white-hot rage. "Get out of here! You were a loser when I first saw you, and you're still a loser! You're pathetic. A nobody. The monks don't want you at *Gakiji* and *Gennan* doesn't have any more time to waste on you!"

"What are you talking about? Roshi and the others never said they didn't want me!" Taro cried.

"Get out of here and stop bothering people. Show some self-respect!" The vitriol spewed out of Ratzitzu's mouth and he couldn't stop, even if he had wanted to. His jealousy and bitterness completely consumed him.

"You think you're special. You're not! You're pitiful. You're a joke in the Temple. A waste of *Gennan's* time and effort. Some first born you turned out to be. Go home and let your baby sister Sachi take care of you."

"Sa . . . Sachi?" Taro was stunned to hear his sister's name.

Ratzitzu was pushing and pushing against this cat, using every bit of information he had heard in Taro's *dokusans* with Roshi. Taro could not have been caught at a weaker moment. And Ratzitzu knew it. He was starting to taste Taro's ruination.

"Who are you and why are you saying these things to me? Stop saying my sister's name!"

As the rat's words beat down on him, Taro struggled to stand up against the assault.

And then a question, so sickening, began to form in Taro's head. *If the rat has been spying on me all along, how could Roshi not have known about this? Was I being deceived by Roshi all this time? Was this the plan from the beginning? Was the rat somehow an assistant to Roshi?*

Taro's breathing turned shallow and rapid as he felt the weight of his doubt and despair begin to crush him. He became dizzy as he fought to defend himself against the rat's aggression and the fear that was building in his head about Roshi.

Ratzitzu saw the opening. "Leave!" he screamed at Taro. "You're not cut out for this. There's nothing for you here. *Gennan* is done with you! You failed!"

Ratzitzu's fuse had finally detonated. He was so angry that this aggravating cat was just standing there, staring at him. "Why are you still here? What don't you understand? Get out!" Ratzitzu shrieked.

Taro was defenseless against the onslaught, but the words thrown at him were not unfamiliar. His Reasonable Mind lurked in the background and smiled. *You see, Taro? You should have listened to me and stayed home. There would have been no yelling, no upset. Nice and easy. Now you've got bigger problems. Will your mother take you back? What was Roshi's relationship with the rat? And did Roshi ever really care?*

A sick, desperate feeling came over Taro as he started to pant and then heave. His relationship with his mother was destroyed and now his chances with Roshi were ruined.

Taro had nowhere to go. When that realization took hold, he turned away from Ratzitzu and slowly slunk off, heading away from the Temple. Head down, his body sagged, belly dragging on the ground.

CHAPTER *Eight*

HAVING MADE it safely back to the forest, the three birds returned for the night to the cluster of cherry trees where they were assured of some birdseed. Later, roosting on one of the lower cherry branches, they were startled awake by unfamiliar noises. Looking down, they saw a rat. He stood up on his hind legs, taunting Taro. *What was Taro doing in the forest so late at night?* they wondered. They dipped their heads down for a closer listen.

Something was wrong. Taro appeared to be suffering.

"Look!" Hiroto said, fluttering his wings, "Taro's walking away from the Temple. He's going in the wrong direction! Come on! I'll take Taro. You two take the rat."

Swooping down, Hiroto flew up in Taro's face, causing him to stop.

"Hey! What are you doing? Go away! Leave me alone!" Taro held up his paws to protect himself from the bird's flapping wings.

The other two birds attacked Ratzitzu by fluttering their wings in his face and pecking at his head and body. They dive bombed him high, then low, then high again from all angles.

Ratzitzu fought back viciously, flailing his arms, running in circles, and snapping his teeth at the air, hoping he would grab onto one of the birds and injure it. Anything to get them away from him.

The birds finally drove him off, and he fled towards the Temple.

Ratzitzu didn't know what had caused the birds to go insane, but he believed another one had also attacked Taro. Good! Great news. Ratzitzu didn't have to be the one to drive Taro out of the forest. A crazy bird could do the job just as well.

Taro could make out the blackbird, even though his shiny black feathers were obscured in the dark of night. He remembered their first encounter. It had been friendly, so Taro didn't understand why the bird was flapping his wings in his face now. "What do you want? Why are you here? Leave me alone!" Taro screamed.

The two cardinals joined Hiroto, and the trio fluttered around Taro's head.

"Taro," Remi said. "Who was that?"

"I don't know. He said his name was something like Ratootsi, Ratzootsuit. Something like that. He's been spying on me!"

"I told you two that rat was trouble!" shrieked Remi, looking at her companions.

"You knew he was here?" asked Taro, a feeling of betrayal sweeping over him again.

"Well, yes and no. I was the first one to see the rat under the Temple's kitchen, but we had no idea what he was doing. Honest! Momo confirmed he was there, that's all," said Remi, hopping around, hoping Taro wouldn't get mad and try to hurt her.

"Ratzitzu!"

"What?" the birds asked altogether.

"Ratzitzu. Now I remember. That's what he said his name was!"

The confusing evening seemed to overflow with too much information.

Taro hesitated, then took a deep breath. He finally asked, "Did Roshi know about the rat?" He crossed his paws in prayer and waited for their answer.

"Of course!" Remi said. "Roshi knows everything. And anyway, we told him because Momo confirmed it for us. But since the rat is still around, then Roshi has a reason for that. He'll eventually use the rat in some way for the good of something. You'll see. Yes, he knows the rat is here."

"But you don't think Roshi and the rat were working together against me, do you?" Taro asked cautiously.

"Oh my God, no. Never!" Hiroto reassured Taro. "There was never any collusion. Roshi knows exactly what he's doing. Remi already said it. He's using the rat for some purpose that we don't know about yet."

Feeling some relief that Roshi probably had not betrayed him after all, Taro said, "But the rat knew so much! He even knew my sister's name," Taro said.

"Maybe he's been watching you, trying to learn from you. To learn how to be a proper Zen student," said Genji.

"What!?" Taro, Remi, and Hiroto said in unison, turning to look at Genji as if he had gone mad. He shrugged and gave a little chirp.

"No, that's not right," said Taro. "He used the information against me."

"Well, obviously he wanted you gone. But listen. The only thing we know is that we don't know what the rat is doing and why he's here. So let's consider some options," suggested Hiroto.

As the four talked and wondered, thought and speculated, the ease of their friendship began to deepen. And within the space of that, it was Remi who finally said what everyone was thinking.

"Taro! It's time to get your butt back to the Temple! You wanted to do this Zen thing. Now go back."

Aligned, the three birds demanded, "Go back, Taro!" flapping their wings in his face again.

Taro covered his eyes from their feathers. "But I can't do it. I don't know how to work with Roshi. And I don't understand *kōans* or what I'm supposed to do. Even the rat knew . . ."

"Stop it!" Hiroto shrieked. "Trust yourself and stop listening to others' opinions. This training is for you, no one else. Now, get off your pity paws!"

"You're a threat for some reason to the rat! That's why he wants you gone. Can't you see that?" Remi demanded.

"Yeah!" exclaimed Genji. "A threat!"

"You were given to us as an inspiration. Look at you! What kind of cat goes into a Zen monastery to train to be a monk?" The birds were fluttering so close around Taro's head, he didn't know who was talking. He put his paws down.

"Come on, Taro. Come on. Choose! What's it going to be?" The birds continued, talking over each other so badly now, they had become unintelligible.

Their belief in him, though, began to renew Taro's determination and commitment to himself. "Did you really mean it when you said I was an inspiration?" he asked.

Remi turned to Hiroto and Genji for confirmation. Then she turned her head back, regarded Taro, and said, "Yes. We meant that from the bottom of our hearts. You inspire us."

After a brief moment, Taro turned around and walked back towards the entrance of the Temple, three noisy birds encouraging him with their flapping wings, the female riding atop his head. They believed in him and refused to give up on him. And so neither would he.

At the Temple gate, Taro stopped and turned. "Thank you for your faith in me and for helping me get back on track." He felt very humbled as he gave each one a soft rub on the top of its head. Then, bowing to them with sincere gratitude, he turned and walked through the gate and back into the *zendo*.

Taro vowed to sit in earnest through the night with his *kōan* and inquire into his original face before his father was born.

The twins, Ben and Ren, witnessed the entire unfolding of the evening from a short distance. They would have stepped in if the birds had not been so quick to respond to Taro and the rat. But when they saw the situation was under control, they held back.

"You can't do this by yourself," Ben mused as he watched Taro turn around and head back to the Temple with the birds.

Ren looked at his twin. "Can't do what by yourself? What are you talking about?"

"Zen training. The student has to hit a wall, has to be driven to quit. It's part of the process. The birds provided Taro a ramp back onto himself. They stood for his commitment until he had the confidence to do it himself. That's how he was able to turn back to the Temple. Now Roshi will see if Taro has the steel to continue."

"It's definitely not for the faint of heart," said Ren.

"No, it's not. Roshi can drive his students to insanity, but if they come out the other side, he may find them worth investing in."

"Uuf!"

"Yeah, Taro is right in the heart of it now. It could go either way," said Ben.

"Hey! Wanna take bets if long tail makes it through or not? The mushrooms are looking pretty good this time of year. Loser picks 15 for the winner," said Ren.

"I would hate to bet against Taro. I'll tell you what. Let's just see if the cat can do this. Most humans fail, but I think Taro is remarkable," said Ben.

Gennan Roshi, in his typical fashion, snuck down to the kitchen to grab a midnight snack, noting on his way that several monks and novitiates occupied the *zendo.* He smiled when he saw Taro on his cushion, and sent a quick thanks to the heavens. It was a major accomplishment of Taro's to move beyond the force that propelled him out the Temple gate earlier. Roshi knew exactly what that was like from his own experience. Many leave. Few return.

Roshi knew after Taro bolted out of his *dokusan* room that Ratzitzu would not be far behind, but he didn't know the birds were the ones responsible for recovering him and escorting Taro back from the forest until he heard their flurry of tooting and whistling at the Temple gate. Evidently they had gotten to Taro before *Daishin* could find him. That was good on two counts. He wanted Taro to feel more connected to the forest and the creatures who inhabited it. And, it was good news to know the birds were back from the village.

By 6:00 a.m. the following morning, the all-night sitting had gotten Taro to an emptied-out place. He had no thoughts or ideas left in him. He didn't even possess any feelings. His attachment to an outcome was no longer precious to him. He had settled into a deep, still place where his breathing kept him grounded to his cushion. His hearing was so sensitive, he could hear the candle flickering on the main altar, the incense ash falling into the bowl.

Sesshin was nearing an end and the *dokusan* line was called early. *Daishin,* having seen Taro sitting through the night in the *zendo,* was relieved and grateful. He went over and tapped Taro lightly on the head. "You're up," he whispered. "Roshi wants to see you."

The tap on his head was enough to bring Taro back to the reality of the *zendo* and his physical body. He yawned and did a long cat stretch to loosen up before moving quickly to the *dokusan* line. When he heard Roshi's bell, he struck the *kansho* with precision and entered the room.

Roshi sat exactly as he had during the previous evening. Nothing had changed. Overcome with relief at seeing Roshi again, and knowing he had not banned him from the Temple, Taro bowed deeply before approaching his teacher.

Looking at him squarely, *Gennan* Roshi said softly, "Taro, show me your original face before your father was born."

And Taro, realizing how drained he had become from the all-night sitting, yawned again. Rubbing his eyes with his paws, he shook his head. "I don't know, Roshi. I really don't know. I'm just so tired right now."

Gennan Roshi yawned widely, rubbed his eyes with his hands, and shook his head.

Taro recognized something deeply familiar in Roshi's movements. As if Roshi were holding a lantern in the fog to show him the path ahead, but Taro couldn't quite make the connection. He looked at Roshi in a confused way and cocked his head.

Roshi looked at Taro in a confused way and cocked his head.

Taro exhaled a deep sigh.

Roshi exhaled a deep sigh.

And then, in that mirrored instant, Taro's brain completely rewired and all that was inaccessible within him surfaced to be seen and understood. And he started to laugh.

And *Gennan* Roshi laughed, too.

Taro had seen the original face, and Roshi had recognized this awakening.

Testing his experience, Roshi prodded, "Before any concepts, before any thoughts, before you think or feel, show me this original face."

Taro yawned again.

"What do words such as *before, father, face, born* mean?" Roshi continued.

"Um . . . uh . . . before any thoughts? They're just concepts. Before I think the thought that there's a face . . . um . . . there's just this?" And Taro licked his paw and rubbed it across his whiskers.

"How tall is this original face, Taro?"

Taro hesitated then stood up.

"How old is this original face?"

"Forever," Taro replied quickly.

"No! Be specific!" Roshi demanded.

"Oh. Three years old."

"And Taro, what did you call this original face when you were a year old?" Roshi asked gently.

And suddenly, Taro understood. With no thought, he said, "Papa." And he started to cry.

"That's right, Taro," Roshi said. "Your father is the original face, too. You are your father. There's nothing but the original face.

"To us, sometimes, we might call it God," Roshi continued. "But there's never anything but the original face. It's not determined by time, or space, or words like *original, father, face, before, born*. These are all just concepts. But now you've begun to discover the domain that will allow you to access something much greater than what you think or know.

"Show me how you can sit on your original face before your parents were born," Roshi continued with a smile.

Taro paused, then got up, fluffed his cushion, and sat back down on it.

Gennan Roshi continued. "Before any concepts are born, this is what we call *emptiness*. It is what all great teachers have discovered. The world before words. As soon as the world was turned into a noun, it gave rise to the illusion of a subject versus an object. A separate self."

"I've spent all this time running from my father, when all along I've been nothing but my father," Taro cried.

Gennan Roshi paused. "Yes. You were so busy not being your father, that you gave up being your true Self, your original Self, which is the whole universe."

Taro fell into *Gennan* Roshi's lap with a mixture of joy and tears, saying, "I didn't know. I just didn't know. I couldn't see it."

Roshi patted Taro's side and rubbed his head. Taro began to purr. "You were born for a purpose larger than yourself. You have something to offer that can contribute to the entire world. To become useful to the planet. To make the world work for yourself and others. Think on this point. Your purpose will take shape over time. Now sit up straight."

Taro sat up and looked at *Gennan* Roshi with such love and gratitude, even Roshi was moved. "Taro, you've had an opening and now you have to deepen and integrate this understanding into your life. This is just the beginning. Others will recognize this in you. Now go back to your seat, sit with this, and inquire even more deeply into this original face. Keep going." *Ding-a-ling-a-ling.*

Daishin noticed the change when Taro returned to his place in the *zendo*. Walking up to him from behind, he gave Taro a gentle squeeze at the scruff of his neck, leaned in, and said softly, "Congratulations."

In the corner of the *dokusan* room, Ratzitzu was apoplectic. He could barely breathe. When he saw the birds bringing Taro back and that one lunatic riding on top of the idiot cat's head, Ratzitzu went bonkers. He thought about attacking Taro in the *zendo* while he was all cool and calm, acting like he knew something about Zen. *What a dope!* But Ratzitzu had to be very alert not to expose himself too much. So now, here he was again, back in the *dokusan* room with *Gennan* blabbering on and on about emptiness and faces everywhere and Taro getting all dewy-eyed. He even had the audacity to fall into *Gennan's* lap! *Yuck! That whole scene was disgusting,* Ratzitzu thought as he popped two in the corner.

CHAPTER *Nine*

TARO'S GLIMPSE into realization was like light shining through a pinhole prick in a black curtain. It was just the beginning, but it fueled a determination to deepen the possibility he had begun to taste with *Gennan* Roshi. New feelings and sensations were eroding everything Taro knew and believed. He felt as if he had just awakened from a monotonous dream. Everything looked different and, for the first time in his life, Taro felt the warmth of love flooding his body - just because. There was a radiance to everything he saw. He was profoundly happy.

Gennan Roshi knew that this inner glow Taro was experiencing would need much more training and practice before he could own it as his own. It also carried with it a high price. If his awakening continued, Taro would eventually have to come down from the mountain of enlightenment and give it all away.

Following the end of *sesshin*, Taro's daily duties in the monastery continued in the kitchen, although he had been removed from dishwashing, and was now officially responsible for stocking and overseeing the food moving in and out of the large pantries, sweeping the kitchen floors, and keeping the pantries clean. So naturally, he was annoyed by the turds that kept piling up in the corner of the largest pantry that held the grains and some of the fruits and vegetables. Initially, Taro assumed it was a natural consequence of living in the forest, even though he hated seeing the poops so close to the food. What else could he do but continue to sweep the pantries clean every day.

However, after his glimpse into enlightenment, life for Taro in the kitchen now felt free from constraints. He approached his responsibilities with satisfaction. Every action naturally flowed into the next with precision and beauty. Turds in the corner of the pantry did not bother him that much any longer. In fact, he often found he welcomed them with curiosity, wondering who they had belonged to.

And yet, despite all of that, Taro knew that something was incomplete for him. He knew there was a missing piece to his fulfillment, and he believed it had to do with his parents.

Making a personal request of Roshi the next time Taro entered *dokusan*, he said, "I feel I have more to say to my parents. Is it possible that I do, Roshi?"

Gennan Roshi smiled. Under the guidance of his teaching, his students understood the power of acknowledging their parents. There was much Roshi could teach Taro in this way. Looking at Taro, he said, "Yes, there is more to say, and I will help you. What are their names?"

"My father's name was Jin, and my mother's name is Reiko."

Gennan Roshi looked at Taro. "I will make a plaque for both your father and mother, even though your mother is still alive. Ask *Daishin* to place you first in line tomorrow morning, and I will help you complete the past with your parents."

Taro bowed deeply to *Gennan* Roshi and left the *dokusan* room, Roshi's bell trailing behind him. *Ding-a-ling-a-ling.*

The next morning, Taro entered the *dokusan* room at 6:00 a.m. and saw there were two plaques with his parents' names placed on the small altar in Roshi's room. The candle was lit and *Daishin* had left a fresh stick of incense burning. There was a box, the *hako*, on the front center of the altar filled with tamped-down ash. Atop the ash was a round charcoal briquette glowing hot orange around the edges. In a separate section of the *hako* to the right of the ash was a small mound of powdered incense. Taro smelled the ancient, woody scent of the ash and incense combination and felt a trace of the briquette's warmth as he approached *Gennan* Roshi and sat down.

Roshi looked earnestly at Taro, who returned his gaze with wide, trusting eyes. Roshi began, "Taro, to truly honor your parents beyond their personalities and shortcomings, you start by giving up the right to punish them. You must be able to elevate them to the level of sainthood."

"I don't understand, Roshi."

"It means, when you can recognize the three miracles your parents performed on your behalf, you will be able to honor them by humbly requesting their forgiveness. The pieces will come together and you will be free from the burden of your past."

"Roshi, what are these three miracles?"

Gennan Roshi paused. "The first is, your mother gave birth to you. That is its own miracle. The second miracle is your parents let you live. They didn't have to. Your mother and father could have abandoned you. There was nothing written that said they had to keep you alive. And the third miracle is that they cared for you until you could care for yourself. Both your mother and father loved you enough to nourish, feed, and care for you until you could do it on your own."

Taro was silent for a moment. "I never thought about it that way, Roshi."

Gennan Roshi nodded. "Now you know."

"What do I do now, Roshi?"

Gennan Roshi said, "Come to the altar, Taro. Here you see the two plaques I made with your parents' names on them. Start now with three full bows of appreciation to each parent." Roshi waited for Taro to complete his bows to his parents as he sprinkled a few pinches of powdered incense onto the charcoal briquette in the *hako*. Wisps of smoke rose up and sanctified the space. "Now, start by speaking what you have to say to your father as if he were here in front of you."

Watching the smoke rise, Taro turned to the simple plaque with his father's name on it and found himself speechless, overcome with emotion.

"Taro, think about what you need to apologize for. What do you need to request your father's forgiveness for?" Roshi said.

Taro was silent for a moment. He felt so sad, even his ears flattened out. He knew. Looking directly at the plaque with his father's name, he said, "Papa, I beg your forgiveness. When you died, I only thought of myself and how I felt my life was not my own anymore. I hated being first born. I felt crushed by that burden. My whole life I ran from you. I never wanted to be like you. I felt restricted by your presence. It was even worse when you died, because then I felt imprisoned by the expectation to be you."

Taro felt so overcome, he stopped. Roshi sprinkled a few more pinches of incense into the *hako* as he waited silently for Taro.

"I tried my whole life not to be you, Papa, but now I realize I am nothing other than you. In my hateful judgment, I missed the chance to really be with you when you were here. I miss you so much. Please forgive me for running from you and for throwing away the love you always had for me. I'm so sorry."

Roshi leaned over, dropped a few more pinches of powdered incense onto the charcoal and waited. Finally, he asked, "Taro, what would you like to say to your mother?"

Taro turned his head to the plaque with his mother's name on it. He thought about the last time he had seen her, how angry she had been when she realized he was leaving. His ears twitched and his tail swished side to side. Taking a deep breath, Taro began. "Mama, I lied to you the whole time after Papa died.

You thought I was the one responsible for bringing home the food, but it was Sachi who did all the work. Before we came home, she always gave me the food to give to you. I never taught her anything. When I brought home that bag of buttons, I wanted to give you something that I had gotten by myself. I was so hurt when you told me they couldn't feed the family because they weren't food. I wanted you to like the buttons because I liked them and I thought they were beautiful. When you were so disappointed, I felt like a failure. So I told myself it was your fault that I felt that way. Mama, please forgive me for blaming you. All you ever wanted was to care for me and our family and make sure we had something to eat. I'm sorry. I miss you so much."

And with that, Taro began to cry.

From his place in the far corner of the *dokusan* room, Ratzitzu stood up on his hind legs and rubbed his eyes. Those stupid blah-blah sob stories! He hated them. His eyes were all wet, and he hated that, too. Then he suddenly understood! Cursing *Gennan* Roshi under his breath, he narrowed his damp eyes. *You idiot Zen teacher! Don't you know that using powdered incense in such a small room is bad for you? It stings your eyes and makes them water!*

Before he rang in his next student, *Gennan* Roshi thought about what he had just heard. Everything was settling into place except Taro's comment about the buttons. Glancing at the corner, Roshi wondered if the rat was there. He made a mental note to go back to the cherry tree to call on the birds. Maybe they could provide a clue. *Just a few more students* he thought, *then I'll head out with some fresh birdseed.*

Gennan Roshi stepped beyond the Temple gate into the forest and drew in a deep breath. He loved this time of year. Winter was melting into spring. It was a magical time of transition with baby buds beginning to delicately poke their heads through thin layers of the last vestiges of snow. Color was starting to return to the forest and Roshi would soon be able to change into lighter robes. Everything began to feel uplifted. There was a vitality in the air, and it brought hope and optimism with it. New babies would soon be born into the forest. And all Roshi had to do was wait. Spring would come all by itself.

Under the branches of a cherry tree, *Gennan* Roshi sat in *zazen*, silently calling the birds to him. Within minutes, he heard the familiar sounds of playfully flapping wings and throaty chirps as the three flew to the closest branch. Each greeted Roshi with a bow. In turn, Roshi placed his hands together in *gasshō*. Palm to palm, two became one, symbolizing the non-dual nature of things. Raising his fingertips to mid-chest level and with elbows out, he bowed to them from the waist.

Straightening up, he looked at these beautiful birds. "Thank you for coming. I am very grateful to you for recovering Taro and bringing him back from the forest to *Gakiji*. Thank you."

The birds nodded, and Hiroto said, "Roshi, we are committed to Taro's training. Do you know what happened to the rat?"

"Hmmm. I'm not sure," Roshi responded. "Anyway," he said with a wave of his hand "I'm curious to hear of your visit to the village marketplace. Did you find Taro's family?"

The birds became excited, chirping over one another. Finally, Genji pushed himself forward and said, "Roshi, we found Sachi first, and she was so skillful. There are no worries about Taro's family being provided for with Sachi in charge."

Roshi smiled and nodded. "And his mother?"

Hiroto said, "We followed Sachi home. Her mother and the two sisters were there. They ate all the food Sachi brought home, and then the girls went off in separate locations and went to sleep. It looked like one needed some special attention. But then the mother went to a box in the corner. There was a bag that she opened and all these shiny black buttons fell out."

Buttons! thought Roshi, "And?"

"Well," Remi said, "she was lying down, licking them and

holding the buttons close to her. She fell asleep with the buttons."

Roshi nodded.

"And then I dropped the bag of powdered incense at their door," Hiroto said. "She got up right away and opened the bag. She held it to her face and slowly breathed in and purred for a while. But then something happened, because all of a sudden she got more active and started to roll around in the buttons, licking the incense bag."

"What do you make of this?" Roshi asked.

"I think the incense reminded her of Taro in a good way," Remi said.

"She misses him!" Genji blurted out.

And with this news, Roshi smiled broadly. "Well done, my friends," he said. "Thank you for your heartfelt report. This information is of great service to Taro and to me, as well. Here. Please accept this as my way of saying thanks."

Gennan Roshi securely placed a wooden bowl of fresh seeds and nuts in the crook of a branch of the cherry tree. Turning, he said with a wave, "Be well. I will see you again soon."

Ratzitzu was having a bad day. Ever since he was forced to listen to that cat's sad sack apology to his parents, he was wondering about his own family. Ratzitzu was one of a litter of 15, and the litters just kept coming and coming and coming. There was no end to it, and today, he couldn't even count as high as the number of descendants that had been created over how many generations. He was pretty sure some of his own would be included in that number, too. As far as he could tell, rats were all the same. Same color, same size, same shape. It was depressing to look out and see yourself reflected in a horror house of mirrors cracked into a thousand pieces. He had thought working with *Ekō* Roshi would break up that monotony, give him a better view of himself. That had been a bust. But Ratzitzu still had a chance to express his individuality by pitting himself against Taro.

Yeah, yeah, yeah, Ratzitzu thought. *My heart-breaking sob story. So sorry for me.* If Ratzitzu felt any pity for himself, he was well equipped to cut that emotion right off. He didn't even give his own rat's ass. He was only concerned with winning. And in order to win, someone needed to lose. And that loser would be Taro. No doubt about it.

CHAPTER *Ten*

FROM TIME TO TIME, *Gennan* Roshi would conduct informal trainings with his students. These sessions happened spontaneously, either when Roshi found an opening to teach or if a student happened to ask a question that could be expounded upon to deepen his or her understanding. He just loved the dharma, and he also had a terrific sense of humor that really came alive, especially in these informal teachings. That's one of the things that made him such a great teacher.

On this particular day, the monks had just finished their daily work practice. That being complete, some were resting or talking to one another under the canopy of trees in the forest, while some attempted to memorize their *kōans* in preparation for their next opportunity to see Roshi in a private *dōkusan*. Others cooled off, walking along the river that ran through the far end of the forest. There was no attention being paid to the Temple. The physical work was over for the day. It was time to rest.

"Taro, come over here. I want you to see something," *Gennan* Roshi called out to Taro as he noticed him walking past the *zendo*.

Taro stopped at the entrance to the *zendo* and looked in. "What is it, Roshi?"

"Come over here, please."

Taro crossed the *zendo's* threshold, bowed respectfully, and padded over to Roshi, who stood directly in front of Taro's cushion. "Look around, Taro. What do you see?" Roshi asked, beginning his gaze at Taro's cushion and then shifting to looking around the Zendo.

"Ummm. Nothing unusual, Roshi. What am I looking for?"

"Open your eye. What is off in here?"

"My eyes are open, Roshi, and I don't see anything."

"Not those eyes. Your one, true Dharma eye."

"Oh." Taro looked around the *zendo*. He saw evenly spaced and aligned cushions throughout the large room. They were plumped and centered on their mats in perfect rows. There was symmetry and balance on the altar, with the flowers and candle just the right height in relation to the bronze Buddha statue elevated in the middle. The ash in the incense bowl at the front of the altar was clean, tamped down, and ready for the next period of *zazen*. All corners in the room were free of cobwebs and the floor was polished to a high sheen.

"I don't see anything, Roshi," said Taro.

"Well then, look within your own space."

Taro looked down and finally understood. "Oh! I see a little ball of cat hair on my cushion.

"And? What about that?"

"It doesn't belong here, Roshi," Taro said as he picked up the wad of fur and tried to tuck it back into himself.

Roshi smiled as he retrieved the fluff from Taro's side and stuck it in his long sleeve, to be thrown away later. "And now what are you left with, Taro?"

Oftentimes when the animals in the forest heard Roshi talking, they would gather nearby to listen in. They thought his informal teachings were worthwhile to their lives, as well. Today proved to be no exception. Well, except for one.

Ratzitzu, burrowed down in the high grass, was lurking in the background, hoping to see another fail on Taro's part. Above, the three birds chirped in greeting to one another and settled down on a branch in front of an open window, waiting for Roshi's teaching with Taro to continue.

"So," Roshi said to Taro. "Now that you've gotten the cat hair off your cushion, what are you left with?"

"I'm not sure I understand, Roshi."

"What is your sense of the *zendo* now that you've picked up the fur? How does it feel in here?"

"It feels maybe a little lighter. That it's appropriate for the fur to be gone. That picking it up was an action that needed to happen. After noticing it, it bothered me. Now the *zendo* seems right. It feels clean and right."

"Yes, Taro. Our practice isn't about adding something to anything. It's about taking away things that don't work any longer. To put things in their proper place. Fur belongs on the cat, not on the cushion.

"A cushion in the *zendo* without fur lives in a state of *impeccability*. You could call it the natural order of things or the way things are supposed to be. Suffering exists because people have balls of fur in their heads and think that's reality. We live in a world full of these balls of fur," Roshi said.

"Do I have fur balls in my head, Roshi?"

"Of course you do, Taro. "

"What about you, Roshi? Do you have them, too?"

"Yes, sometimes. Of course. What do you think the fur balls are that live in your head that keep you from seeing the true nature of things?"

"I don't know, Roshi. I can't think. I'm worried about having fur balls in my head."

"Taro," Roshi said, laughing, "the *fur* is a metaphor for, say, the three poisons – greed, anger, and ignorance. Or it could represent resignation, delusion, jealousy. These are the fur balls I'm referring to. These types of states of mind are what get in our way of seeing the truth of reality."

"Oh. What does it take to get rid of this fur in my head, Roshi?" Taro asked.

"Most people say they want freedom, but they don't want to look at these wads of fur in their heads.

"I do!"

"Well then, maybe a teacher could point you in the direction of reality."

"Will you be my teacher, Roshi?" Taro blurted out, momentarily forgetting *Gennan* Roshi already was his teacher.

"Yes, if you'll be my teacher," Roshi said as he smiled and bowed at the waist to Taro. "*Impeccability* is an important lesson for you to learn as a student in training. Now you can begin to see that reality will always tell you what's going on. In this case, reality is your true teacher. For example, when you understood that the fluff of fur didn't belong on your cushion, you removed it and imbued the room with *impeccability*."

At this point, the birds looked at one another and shrugged. Remi leaned into them. "Good Lord. What is he talking about? We invented pecking!"

"Yeah," said Genji. "That's pretty much all we do when we're not flying Roshi missions. We're pecking. Peck, peck, peck, peck, peck."

"So I guess that means we're already impeccable!" cried Hiroto as the three birds took off in unison, their laughter trailing behind them.

Roshi and Taro looked up as the three lovable birds flew off. But Ratzitzu stayed grounded in the high grass.

"One last piece of training for today, Taro," said Roshi. "What allows for this state of *impeccability* to appear?"

"Gee, Roshi. I'm not sure. Willingness? Curiosity? Maybe awareness?"

"Not exactly. Think. What gives rise to *impeccability*?"

"I guess I don't know, Roshi."

"It's *care*. You have to care. When caring is brought forth, you have the possibility of being *impeccable*. And once you can see it, it's everywhere. But you also have to be able to see where it's not. You can tell what reflects your lack of caring. There's no harmony or appreciation present."

Taro looked at Roshi with wide eyes. He had a lot to learn.

"And now, Taro, let's go take a look at your room."

Ratzitzu hung back in the grass. *Adios you two and sayonara, fools!* He didn't care about Taro's room. He was thinking about those three psycho birds and what they had just said. *You know what? I'm impeccable, too,* he thought, scratching his butt. *Sure, of course I am. Because I care. I care a* **lot** *that soon this orange stooge is going to be out of here, and hey, I see that care reflected everywhere. No lack of caring over here. No, sir. Impeccability abounds.* Ratzitzu stood tall, saluted, and pooped in the grass.

CHAPTER *Eleven*

THE BLESSING of the Animals Ceremony was a ritual *Gennan* Roshi had performed for as many springs as he and his monks had lived in the forest. It represented a critical extension of his appreciation towards the animals and an outward sign of his own values. The value he placed on the ceremony was one of utter importance. The ceremony offered what Roshi thought of as a reciprocal gift, with no distinction between giver and receiver.

But now, Roshi needed to mentally prepare for the ceremony. Calling Taro and *Daishin* into his *dokusan* room, Roshi said, "This year, I'd like to do the Blessing of the Animals at the end of May, during this year's peak bloom season. That should give the new mamas and papas enough time to gather their babies and attend. *Daishin,* I need you to announce the information to the old oak that guards the forest. The wind and other trees will take care of the rest."

Daishin understood perfectly. He bowed and left.

Gennan Roshi then turned to Taro. "We forget how profound and miraculous life is. We forget to appreciate what we have. This Blessing is based around gratitude, and the ceremony helps us to remember to stay in harmony with all things. It reminds us of who we are as we attempt to express the inexpressible." Even if Roshi could not put into words the significance of what this ceremony meant to him, he believed it when he said, "As long as you get the spirit right, the rest will fall into place."

Taro nodded and started to purr. He loved listening to Roshi.

Roshi continued, "There are elements of our common being, animals and people alike, that you will see represented in the ceremony. I will speak more directly about these elements when it's time."

Taro was transfixed. Never had he expected to be brought in so closely to the Animal Blessing Ceremony. What he had originally thought of as just a gathering of the animals in the forest with a prayer or a chant from Roshi was nothing like that at all. These creatures, dead or alive, were all being equally honored. This was a big deal to Roshi, and he held it with grave significance. He had stamped his importance on it. And so would Taro.

From his corner in the *dokusan* room, Ratzitzu munched on an orange as he listened to Roshi rattle on about an animal blessing ceremony that was to happen soon. *Honk shoo. Another boring snoozefest ceremony with Gennan at the helm, no doubt. But, hey! Why not attend? What else is there to do?* Of course, Ratzitzu wasn't part of the forest community, *thank God* he always thought. And he dared not show his face again yet, but maybe this ceremony was something he should at least take advantage of. It might serve him well, maybe even proving *Gennan* would be worth something to him after all.

It would also give him a chance to see that stupid mouse with the white pompadour. He was convinced that she was the one who kept leaving those sticks at the front entrance to his tunnel. Yes, he chewed on them and, yes, his teeth had begun to file down. Still, he didn't trust her. He found her actions intrusive and potentially very dangerous. Although, so far, so good. He didn't believe anyone else in the forest knew the location of his hiding place. But she could blow his cover with one stupid squeak to another animal. And yet, he was disappointed when there were no sticks waiting for him at the entrance to his tunnel. He hated that he hated that.

The day of the Animal Blessing was spring-perfect, with a refreshing breeze and puffy clouds scattered throughout the sky. Several hours before the beginning of the ceremony, two monks brought out a low table, Roshi's sitting cushion, and his bowing mat, placing them under the majestic oak tree. This old oak would oversee the Blessing of the Animals and shelter Roshi as well. As the forest's guardian, the oak was proud and dignified, and had presided over this ceremony with Roshi from the beginning. It was the tree's duty and his pleasure to safeguard everything that happened underneath his protective watch and covering.

Daishin approached the low table that would become the altar. He carefully draped a purple cloth with golden thread weavings over the table. Then, organizing everything to face Roshi, he placed a *hako* directly in the center of the table with an unlighted charcoal briquette in the center of the tamped down ash, making sure there was a nice pile of powdered incense in the box as well.

To the left of the hako, he placed a plain vase with a small, beautiful bouquet of buttercups offered up from the forest. To the right of the hako, he placed a white candle that would remain unlit throughout the ceremony. It was representative only, as the monks would never endanger the forest with a burning flame. Finally, directly in front of the *hako*, for Roshi's easy reach, was a small brass cup filled half-way with water, across which was a cut-off pine bough of about three inches, its branch covered in twine.

Roshi's sitting cushion was carefully placed directly in front of the table, where everything was easily accessible. Finally, moving to the other side of the table, *Daishin* laid Roshi's bowing mat down, far enough away from the altar so as not to hit his head when performing three full bows. A hand hammered bronze gong had already been brought out, and *Daishin* carefully placed a conch on the ground near the gong. Looking around, he appeared satisfied.

Raising his head to take in the beautiful oak, *Daishin* reverently touched the tree's trunk. With profound respect, he breathed in. The oak was the guardian of the forest. The most fortunate of small animals and insects had already taken up residence in its gnarly roots, crannies, and crevices. *Daishin* loved this ancient tree, just as he loved every aspect of the forest. Hating to leave but knowing it was time, he finally said, "Guard well all that is beneath you. And thank you, as always, for your kind and lasting service." The leaves on the branches of the oak fluttered gently in a sudden breeze.

The animals of the forest had been making their way to the old oak, starting out early enough to move their babies along while giving themselves sufficient time to get seats as close to the front as possible. In their excitement, they noisily announced themselves as they approached their destination. Some of the younger animals were jumping and hopping up and down, the birds were happily gliding in long, low arcs across the sky. Even the smallest insects seemed larger as they sat or stood at full attention.

Everything on the forest floor, including the leaves, grasses, rocks, vines, tree roots, and moss, provided seats for the animals. From up above, the three birds saw their community form a stunning mosaic. Soon the humans would become a part of the pattern. This Blessing was an opportunity for all creatures to join with one another. And, Roshi always threw a great party afterwards, which held its own appeal.

Gennan Roshi, dressed in his ceremonial robes, was ready to make his way down to the altar under the oak. "Go now, Taro," Roshi said. "The animals of the forest would like you to join them in being blessed today. Sit with them, meet them, relax, and enjoy what good fortune comes to all of us."

Preparations on Roshi's end were all in order. A junior monk had already gone to the altar and lit the charcoal briquette in the *hako*. It would be his sole responsibility to keep a watchful eye on that briquette until it was wetted down, covered in dirt, and buried deep in the ground at the end of the ceremony.

At 10:00 a.m. a monk picked up the conch and exhaled a long, deep breath into it, announcing the beginning of the Animal Blessing Ceremony. The gong, slowly struck three times, sent out waves of vibrations that penetrated the wind and lingered within the bodies of everyone.

Ratzitzu's eyes poked out from some woody vegetation far to the rear of the last row in the group. He was ready to bolt if he had to, but he doubted he'd need to. Everyone had eyes only for Roshi. It was foolish on their part, he felt, but he would keep watching as long as the boredom didn't kill him.

Gennan Roshi approached the altar through rows formed on either side, allowing him a clear path to his bowing mat. From there, he completed three full bows before walking around to the other side of the altar, where he sat down facing the animals. He picked up a pinch of powdered incense from the *hako*, dropped it on the heated briquette, and briefly watched as smoke rose up and was carried away on the breeze.

Scanning the group from high up in the sky, then deep into the ground nearby, to far out beyond the last row, Roshi smiled. Taking his time, he made eye contact with as many creatures as he could.

"Good morning. Thank you for being here. It has been a privilege for the monks and me to be allowed to share your home in the forest. For centuries you have welcomed us and taught us, and we remain forever your humble servants. This blessing is offered in gratitude.

"We begin by honoring those who have left us this past year."

Roshi dropped another, slightly larger pinch of powdered incense into the *hako* and again, the smoke rose up. "The smoke of this incense is here for a while and then it disappears, reflecting the temporary nature of all things, of all our lives. Life is itself impermanent. Without this impermanence, there can be no life."

He sprinkled another, smaller pinch of incense on the coal. "To all who have gone before us in this past year, you were our gracious teachers. Through your passing, we are reminded of our universal connection and the pain and grief that cut through the hearts of us all." Roshi placed one more pinch of incense on the coal and made a deep, sitting bow. There was a rustle from many clusters of animals, who also lowered their heads in remembrance.

"No matter what our outward form may be, whether animal or human, we share common elements that are necessary for life. These elements are what we, what all of us, are. We are each of these elements." Roshi motioned to the vase of flowers. "These flowers represent the earth. Mother Earth, who nourishes and sustains us. She gives us everything we need, invites us to sit in her lap of brambles, grasses, flowers, and ferns.

"I bless you with this earth, as solid as your body. Take care of yourselves and be kind, for each of you is a gift."

Oh, my GOD! This is the borefest of the century, thought Ratzitzu. *I can't take your prattle any longer, Gennan. I'm not interested in kindness.* Ratzitzu blew a raspberry. *A gift to me, a gift to you. Blah! Totally overrated. Get over it! Say something worthwhile for a change!* Venturing out cautiously from the brambles, he made his way to as many leftover fallen acorns as he could find and gathered them up. He returned to the wooded area and stashed them in a pile.

Roshi dropped another pinch of powdered incense into the *hako*. Running his hand through the smoke as it rose, he brought it to his nose. "With this air, I bless you. It fluctuates and changes just as you do. Your passions will awaken within you fear and joy, violence and contentment. Your passions are good gifts, and you will know them all. This air element also represents vast space. Always remember that nothing can exist unless there is space for it to be."

Ratzitzu could feel his organs begin to squeeze together, removing whatever space there was left in his body. His intolerance was building.

Roshi motioned to the unlit candle on the altar. "With this fire, I bless you. Of course the briquette is lit," Roshi said, motioning to the *hako*, "because it doesn't produce a flame, yet we envision the flame on the candle. But we never need to light a candle in the forest. Fire represents the heat from the sun, without which we cannot live. And fire also illuminates. Its brightness always leads us home to a safe and predictable place of refuge."

Yeah, yeah, thought Ratzitzu. *How about all of you just go home and be illuminated? Here, take this and this,* he said to himself as he started launching the acorns into the crowd. Several of the animals were hit by the flying acorns and wondered what was happening. A few took advantage of the falling nuts and tried to snack on them before realizing they were old and stale. What was going on? Was the old oak losing it?

Finally, without removing the small cut-off pine branch, Roshi raised the brass cup of water so all could see. "Water is the final element, of which we are mostly made. Water has the power to heal and cleanse and is the medium through which wisdom flows. This pine branch, a natural element, is used to transmit this intangible wisdom."

Holding the brass cup in his left hand, Roshi took the pine

branch and ran it three times from the top of his head down towards his forehead and into the water. On the third time when the pine branch was dipped in the water, Roshi flicked it outward to his left, wetting the heads of some of the animals that were sitting the closest. Then he dipped the branch again in the cup and repeated the process to the right, saying, "Everything I have ever learned from my teacher, from his teacher before him, and up through the lineage, I impart to you. Wisdom is shared selflessly."

And then, in reverse, he dipped the pine branch in the water and ran the branch up backwards from his forehead to the top of his head three times, saying, "And now I take in all the wisdom each of you has imparted to me. This collaborative alchemy produces miracles within each of us. This blessing is a reminder of the wisdom and fleeting nature of our earthly journey. With this, we agree to grow in conscience, take in each moment's lesson, and assume our place within our community and our world. We welcome the new babies who have just begun their journeys on this plane. All of whom have granted us an immeasurable gift. Grow well and be joyous."

Yeah, sure, thought Ratzitzu. *I'll grow well and be joyous when that idiot ginger wannabe finally leaves the forest once and for all. When is this revolving nightmare ever going to end?*

And then Roshi stood. Carrying the small brass cup of water and the pine branch, he moved around the altar and started to make his way down the rows of animals. He dipped the pine branch into the cup of water and touched as many animals on their heads as possible with it, sometimes flicking water out into the crowd. The animals parted to help him make his way through the group. Whenever Roshi saw new babies, or they were offered up to him, he dipped his finger in the water and touched each on the head. When he reached the woody vegetation that butted up against the far end of the group, he made a special effort to shake plenty of water off the pine branch in that direction. Ratzitzu was shocked when several drops of water fell on his head. Not knowing what to make of it, he pooped but remained still until Roshi walked by.

Gennan Roshi continued to bless the animals with the element of water until he had covered every inch of the group that had gathered.

Finally returning to the front of the altar, he poured the remaining water from the brass cup onto the oak tree, and then handed the cup and pine branch to *Daishin*. From his bowing mat in the front of the altar, Roshi made three full bows. Then he stood, made one deep standing bow, backed up and extended his arms out wide, representing an inclusion of all the animals, trees, plants, and monks in the forest. He brought his hands together in a gracious palm to palm *gasshō* and bowed one final time. He looked up and winked at the oak, turned away from the altar, and left the area, making his way back to the Temple gates. The gong was struck slowly three times again. The ancient oak glimmered and shook.

Daishin announced the completion of the Animal Blessing Ceremony. There would be treats and festivities for everyone inside the gates of the *Gakiji* Temple. Come now. All were welcome.

When the water landed on Ratzitzu's head, it sizzled on his skin like bacon in hot grease, and it made him offload a few turds. He wasn't sure what that reaction was all about, but when he realized he had been at the ceremony for hours, he cursed himself for wasting his time. He could have been infinitely more productive digging a longer tunnel to somewhere. And yet it had been fun to see how many animal heads he could hit with the acorns. He even tried getting an acorn into the tumbleweed on top of that absurd field mouse, but it had bounced right off. She probably didn't even feel it.

The creatures of the forest loved the after-party of the Animal Blessing Ceremony. Roshi and his monks laid out a celebratory table full of nuts, fruits, honey, cheese, and fresh water. Animals danced, chirped, squeaked, hooted, croaked, yelped, and sang. They were free and loving life in the forest with Roshi and the monks. Babies fell asleep as the parents and older animals danced and chatted with those they had not seen for a while. Taro was welcomed into the community.

They loved Taro because they loved Roshi.

Momo, the little gray field mouse, approached Taro, her tuft split in several directions. Looking up, she said, "Taro, do you remember me? Do you? You do, right?"

Taro, initially caught off guard, said, "Wait, are you . . .?"

Momo said, "Yes! You almost killed me, but you didn't really! But don't worry. I forgive you! I'm fine. See? We're so happy to have you. Welcome to your new home!"

On hearing the word *home,* Taro realized a level of acceptance that went beyond anything he had ever known. And the word stuck with him. Here he was, being accepted just because. He loved and adored his mother and sisters, of course, yet this new experience transcended the unconditional acceptance of birth family.

Ratzitzu watched the festivities. He had moved from the woody vegetation and now was under some rocks, closer to the gates of the Temple. He saw that silly mouse talking to Taro and wondered what they were saying to one another. *Arch nemeses, the both of them. Neither one to be trusted. So what was this? Were they in cahoots?* All he knew was his suspicions were on the rise with her again. And he now threw Taro into the mix as well. Growing fidgety, he just couldn't relax. What he needed was some of that cheese.

CHAPTER *Twelve*

THE SUMMER BROUGHT its heat and the desire to move at a slower pace, which was why Roshi used this time of year to shake up his students to keep them on their toes. He expected them to stay awake and alert. Changing up summer work assignments was always a good way to train. Some would be elevated in their positions, and some lowered. It all depended. But it wasn't as random as it may have appeared.

Roshi would often say, "You're only as big as you're willing to be small." For him that meant, if you could not be turned on and excited about cleaning the toilets, a foundational step in your training had been missed. He expected his monks to transcend the belief they were entitled to anything. Roshi himself always participated in work practice. Sometimes he would wash the windows. Other times, he would do construction work related to the Temple or manage the trash. It did not matter. Whatever was wanted or needed. The playing field was level. No highs, no lows. Roshi never tolerated students whining they were victims of their circumstances. All monks were included in the work and took equal ownership of the monastery every day.

Some of the monks looked forward to the change that came this time of year. Especially those in the kitchen responsible for stirring enormous boiling cauldrons of water for rice or vegetables as the heat arrived. The hot steam from those pots was welcomed in December. But by July, a monk could not wear enough sweatbands to keep from dripping into the pot. But of course, no monk ever lodged a complaint. They were forever grateful for the opportunity to train with *Gennan* Roshi. Besides, a complaint would have ensured the rest of the summer spent staring into a vortex of scalding water, had they said anything. No, the cooks were quiet. But they, in particular, were always hopeful for reassignment in the summer.

Taro had only known the kitchen since his entrance to *Gakiji* in January. Initially, the head cook had thought of having Taro stir the boiling rice water in the oversized vats, but he worried the cat might fall in.

Gakiji's head cook excelled at his job in the monastery, but he could be equally as grouchy. The real reason he decided against putting Taro near the cauldrons of boiling water didn't involve any concern for the cat's life. Not at all. It was because the monks were all vegetarians. And if the cat fell into the water, that would be such a waste of rice and water, not to mention the time it would take to empty out and clean the vat. And then have to start all over again.

So Taro had been in the pantries for the past six months. They were cool as the days heated up, and he was getting used to the smells of the foods he stocked. He recognized the milky-grain smell of dry rice and the moment when any mold took over. All the vegetables had their own aromas, too, and he knew when to offer them up to the cooks as a nutritious meal or when to inform the head cook their time had ended, which was rare. Surrounded by the summer sweetness of fresh turnips and carrots, the earthy smells of new potatoes, and the vinegar pungency of pickled cucumbers, Taro loved all the kitchen smells. Aware of the turds in the corner, he categorized them under their own particular fragrances and tried to love them, too, before sweeping them away.

Therefore it was no surprise that Taro could not believe it when *Gennan* Roshi told him that his time in the kitchen had come to an end for the summer. Taro was now assigned to the vegetable field to the west of the Temple grounds. He would be overseeing the growing of the squash and tomatoes for the summer.

"Oh, no, Roshi, no. Please," Taro begged. "I'll do anything. Just please don't put me in the vegetable garden to grow food!"

He pressed his paws together in hopeful prayer. Upon hearing that he would be tasked with growing a part of the monks' daily meals, Taro thought back to the days when the weight of his family's well-being - their entire lives - rested on his shoulders. And he recalled his utter failure in that responsibility.

Taro's inadequacy and self-doubt when Roshi reassigned him to the vegetable field infused him with fear. He knew he was no provider. "Please, please, no garden! Anything but that, Roshi, please!"

Gennan Roshi gave Taro his moment. Then, smiling at him, he said, "All new assignments start tomorrow." Turning, he walked away.

Aja, a monk *Gennan* Roshi had ordained several years ago, had also been re-assigned to the vegetable field for the summer, and she soon discovered she would be working alongside Taro. *Aja* had had many cats as a child and, when she was granted acceptance into *Gakiji*, one of the things she missed the most was her big, beautiful boy, Masa. She loved her cat. He was the hardest living being for her to leave when she came to the monastery.

The thought of Taro, who she had known since his Entering Ceremony, triggered longing and many loving feelings within *Aja*. She often found she had to force herself to see Taro as more than a mere Temple cat. He wasn't. He was a cat in serious Zen training. But, oh! It was so hard not to give him scratches behind the ears and tickles under the chin. To carry him around.

When his new work assignment started the next day, Taro arrived at the vegetable garden dragging a shovel behind him, only because he thought that was what was expected. *Aja* laughed when she saw him. "Oh, Taro," she said, reaching out to pet him, then immediately withdrawing her hand. "You're so silly. There's no digging necessary. Everything has already been planted. Look," she said, sweeping her hand across the large patch. "All we have to do is be vigilant and tend what's already growing, remove the weeds, check for bugs, and pick the vegetables when they're ripe."

Taro looked up at *Aja* with relief. As long as she was involved, it would be a good summer. She could train him and, together, they would please the monks with the excellent vegetables they provided. He purred and rubbed up against her leg in gratitude, and *Aja* couldn't resist one little finger stroke across the top of Taro's head.

Ratzitzu, from the vantage point of a nearby tool shed, did a dance. A dance he had made up to thank his lucky stars, the gods, even *Gennan*. He didn't care who got the credit. A dance that said, *I love you, world! You have finally delivered Taro to me!*

Gennan Roshi had predicted Taro would resist the assignment. He knew that tending the vegetables would throw Taro back to his past. And that was exactly what Roshi wanted. He wanted to show Taro that his past was not his present, and it did not dictate his future. He also knew *Aja* would be a good partner for Taro. She was kind and helpful, even though she talked too much. Roshi could overlook that. He was prepared to train Taro in all directions, including whatever came up with that rat that was still lurking around.

"Look over here, Taro," *Aja* said as she placed a straw hat on her head. It was unusually warm. "All the tomatoes are in one place. See them growing on the vines? And over here on this side are several different kinds of squash. We could pick some now if you'll go grab a few baskets." Taro went to the shed closest to the vegetable patch, where gardening tools, fertilizer, hats, gloves, and baskets were stored. Two eyes watched him from behind a tipped over wheelbarrow.

The first week in the garden seemed long. But Taro found it fulfilling. It was Ratzitzu who got bored quickly because all that was happening was the girl was blabbering non-stop and Taro was following instructions like a dog in training. But Ratzitzu was getting the lay of the land. He knew when those two arrived and departed, and who, if anyone, ever came back to the field in the afternoon or evening. Basically, no one.

It looked like clear sailing after Taro and the gabby girl left at the end of each morning. And the location was far enough from the Temple that no one wanted to walk over in the heat unless assigned to work here. Ratzitzu would relax for a few days and let Taro get comfortable with the work as he followed the talking head around. There was plenty of time.

Within two weeks, there were so many vegetables to pick, even *Aja* had little time to chatter. The head cook was very pleased with the crop and the monks all nodded their appreciation to *Aja* and Taro for a job well done. They loved summer vegetables.

The days melted together, but by the end of the third week, Aja became ill with heat exhaustion. She was taken off garden duty until cleared by Roshi to return.

"*Aja*, I can't do this without you," Taro said.

Aja smiled. "You'll be fine, Taro. I just need to stay out of the sun for a few days, and then I'll be back. In the meantime, pick as many vegetables as you can. Just keep doing what we've been doing. I'll be back before you know it. I had asked Roshi if he was going to replace me, but he said you would be fine managing this on your own."

Ratzitzu lounged in the garden shed, contemplating his next move. He chewed on one of the sticks that the little bobblehead mouse was still leaving for him. His smile must look pretty good by now. He didn't see how it would help him be more attractive, or why that was even important, but he chewed the stick anyway as he watched *Aja* stumbling around. *Hey! Reverend Windbag! If you can't take the heat, get out of the vegetable patch. Hahahaha!* And then he watched her leave. Yes! Now was his chance, his teaching moment, as *Ekō* Roshi would have said. The time had arrived.

The sun took forever to go down that day, but when it was dark enough, Ratzitzu ventured out to the garden. Standing alone in the middle of this vast space among the squash and tomatoes, he stood and spread his arms out wide. Turning in a slow circle, he said, "Tomorrow, this will all look different."

Ratzitzu quickly realized that to go deeply into the roots of the squash and tomatoes to kill them entirely would take too long. So he would go broad and superficial to give the illusion of utter destruction. The result would be more devastating to Taro, and ultimately more satisfying to Ratzitzu.

By the time the sun rose the next day, the garden was an out-and-out ruin. Ratzitzu proudly applauded his hard work. Lounging again in the garden shed while munching on a tomato scrap, he anticipated Taro's arrival.

At first, Taro thought the heat was getting to him. He blinked several times when he saw before him the terribly misshapen landscape. Something was different. Picking up his pace, he began to run to the area where, just yesterday, tall tomato plants and robust squash vines had filled this field. His and *Aja's* ground. But now, all he saw were patches of beaten down stalks and twig remnants. Crushed tomatoes, punctured squash, and drying leaves curled in the heat. So many of the beautiful, healthy plants were dying or already dead.

A savage fierceness arose in Taro. An instant feeling of rage that he rarely allowed himself to feel. But this intense fury was beyond his control and grew from a hollow pit in his belly, spread throughout his chest, and exploded in a low, pain-filled cry. The sound shook the woodland creatures so badly, many stopped what they were doing and ran to the forest's periphery to see if their lives were in danger. Ben and Ren, the twin fawns, reached the sidelines first.

Taro was devastated and furious that someone had violated this patch of land he so valued, the place where he and *Aja* had toiled and tended and loved.

And so it was in that moment, Taro lost his mind. Driven by his rage and the guilt and shame of this loss, he began to run. Around and around the patch. He knocked over the remaining stalks that still stood, dug his claws into the dirt as he rounded corners, kicked up baby squash. He decimated what few good tomatoes remained on the ground, and then bruised or ruined younger squash from the hard impact of his body weight. He could not stop running, yowling with anger and sorrow. He kept going, destroying the vegetables more completely with each rotation.

When the three birds heard the cries, they went to find *Gennan* Roshi who, along with *Daishin*, had been digging a compost pit several hundred yards away from the kitchen. They had already dropped their shovels in anticipation of running toward the sound.

Hiroto screeched, "Roshi! Roshi, come quickly! *Daishin*, come! Something's happening in the vegetable field."

They both ran towards the field, the birds way ahead of them. From many yards away, Roshi and *Daishin* saw a storm of dust and dirt kicking up, then settling, then kicking up and settling again around this large mass of land where vegetables had grown. As they approached, they saw a streak of orange running in manic circles around and around the field.

Daishin immediately stepped forward, and shouted, "Taro, stop! Look what you're doing! You're destroying all the vegetables! Stop!"

Taro was so frenzied, he was incapable of stopping.

Gennan Roshi stepped in and shushed *Daishin* with the motion of his hand. Everyone and everything stood still except for Taro. Roshi waited. And he continued to wait until Taro was spent and fell to his side in the middle of the garden. Roshi then approached Taro, kneeled down, ran his hand once down Taro's wet, heaving side, then stopped.

In the distance, the striking of the wooden *han* began, signaling the midday call to *zazen*. The monks had seven minutes to be on their cushions.

Roshi paused. "Get up, Taro. It's time to go sit in the *zendo*."

Taro's eyes momentarily caught Roshi's, but he could not sustain the contact.

Roshi patted Taro lightly once on his side, then stood in response to the call of the *han*. He beckoned to *Daishin,* and the two walked back to the Temple in silence, followed by the three birds. The creatures standing on the edge of the forest receded into the background and returned to their business, although some were not completely convinced they were out of danger.

Before turning away, Ren asked his twin, "What just happened? What's wrong with Taro?"

"Nothing is wrong with him. Something devastated him and it got the better of him," said Ben.

"Really? What could it have been?" asked Ren.

"I don't know, but whatever it was, something cut into him very deeply, like a wound from the past, possibly."

"Yeah, but he went completely off the rails. He almost killed himself running around like that," said Ren.

"You know, Ren, sometimes to be of use, you need that kind

of intense energy to effect change. But this time, Taro only showed up as enraged and unbalanced. His anger just fell back on him," said Ben.

"What does that mean?

"It means anger had our friend in its grip. He was no longer in control of himself and, well, you see what happened. So he's got more work to do."

"Geez. When does it ever end?"

"Never."

Ratzitzu could not believe what he had just seen. The cat had made the problem worse! There was no way in the world Ratzitzu could have predicted that. His heart sang out with joy.

And I can't wait to see you get your fat butt handed to you in dokusan. I hope, I hope that's coming 'cuz Gennan went waaay too soft on you out there. Typical Gennan behavior. Reward the losers. Regardless, Ratzitzu believed he had earned the right to do a victory lap or two around the shed. *Hip hip!!*

When *Gennan* Roshi entered the Temple, he went straight into his *dokusan* room, followed by *Daishin*. After the altar was prepared, Roshi said, "When Taro comes back to the *zendo,* please bring him to me. Otherwise, I will stay here and sit. No students until this afternoon."

Daishin bowed to Roshi and left the room.

Taro missed the first period of *zazen,* but was on his cushion for the second period. *Daishin* immediately tapped him lightly on the top of his head and told him Roshi wanted to see him in *dokusan*.

Once Taro entered the room, he bowed in deep shame to Roshi. He was feeling disgraced and unworthy. But underneath, a brutal anger still simmered and churned in his guts that he couldn't rise above.

Roshi motioned Taro forward with his teaching stick, indicating to take a seat in front of him, which Taro reluctantly took with his head down.

"Why did you stop out there, Taro? There were more vegetables you could have destroyed."

"Roshi, I . . ." Taro faltered.

"Our training here is about doing complete work. But your work out there is not done. You missed a few vegetables you could have gotten good," Roshi taunted.

Taro's pain and anger rose and started to choke him. He sweat as his breathing became heavier, pupils constricted.

"Wait until the head cook hears about this. And what do you think the monks are going to do when they realize they're only getting rice and pickles for lunch, huh?" Roshi jabbed Taro on his side with his stick a few times. "Maybe it's time to quit."

Taro's anger reached its boiling point. A low growl built as his body coiled and hardened. His ears flattened and his tail went rigid.

"And *Aja*? You let her down, didn't you?" Roshi demanded as he planted one end of his stick back down on the ground. "How does that build her trust in you?"

At the mention of *Aja's* name the room spun out from underneath Taro, and he fell headlong into a black abyss. Falling into the void brought with it an unearthly scream. Starting at the tip of his tail, roiling through his guts, and erupting out his mouth like a projectile, Taro's fury and rage exploded like shattered crystal across the room. He arched his back, bared his teeth, and spat at Roshi. His claws swiped close to Roshi's face as he growled and hissed in aggression and fear.

Roshi looked at Taro's claws so close to his face and shrugged. "What are you going to do, Taro? Attack me? Those claws are better used to poke a zucchini."

And with that final insult, Taro lunged and snatched Roshi's teaching stick from his hands. Shaking uncontrollably, breathing erratically, Taro stood to his full height and hurled the stick against the wall with all his force.

Roshi glanced at the wall then looked up at Taro, still standing over him. "Is that your purpose, Taro? Breaking sticks against the wall?"

The *dokusan* room went silent.

Never had Taro regained presence of mind so quickly as he had with Roshi's use of a single word. His *purpose*. The one thing Taro had staked everything on at the risk of losing his family and even his own life. And he had forgotten it all, buried under his pain and rage.

Taro's breathing slowed as his pupils returned to normal. He looked around the room and cringed when he realized what he had done to Roshi's teaching stick.

Roshi remained still.

Taro walked over to the stick lying against the wall. A sizable chunk had broken off from the tip. Taro picked it up off the floor and carried it back to his seat. He laid it in front of his teacher, unable to cover up what he had done to it. Bowing, he said, "I'm sorry, Roshi."

Roshi placed his hand on top of Taro's bowed head and held it there. It was a healing moment generated from *Gennan* Roshi to Taro. Then he picked up his teaching stick, placed the damaged end on the floor and rested his forearm on the other end.

"You've been *doing* nicey-nicey cat on top of all your pain and anger. It's like putting frosting on a cow pie. But now you don't have to *do* nicey-nicey cat. You can actually *be* a nice cat. And what grants you this is the acknowledgment of both sides of yourself. Your anger, this kill energy you have, on one side, and the wisdom and compassion you have on the other side. They go hand in hand. You will find your power, and ultimately your freedom, at the intersection of these two opposites."

Of course the monks, all of whom sat quietly in *zazen*, heard the sounds coming out of the *dokusan* room. Not knowing exactly what was going on or what had been said, many were moved and even inspired by the intense purity of Taro's expression, wishing they had the ability to override their self-consciousness to let it rip that way.

Aja sat in the *zendo*, too, and broke out in tears. She vowed that the next time she saw Taro, she would pick him up and give him a long hug and snuggle. He deserved it, and she didn't care about the hands-off policy.

Ratzitzu, on the other hand, was brought right up to the edge of his sanity. *Why? How? How could you do that, Gennan? You just let that pumpkin schlub get away with busting up vegetables and completely ruining everything! The fact you can't see what a flaming ass loser Taro is, is beyond anything I can wrap my brain around. What is* ***wrong*** *with you?* he screamed in his head.

After seeing his last student, *Gennan* Roshi sat quietly alone in his *dokusan* room, thinking. He realized the morning with Taro had gone in a direction that he could never have previously even considered. Then he turned and focused his eyes on the corner. "Thanks, Ratzitzu," he said. "It's because of you that Taro was able to get to the next level."

Ratzitzu's eyes widened. *No no no no no!* He instantly dumped on the floor, then froze like an ice statue.

CHAPTER *Thirteen*

GENNAN ROSHI SENT *Aja* back to the field, and he appreciated how quickly she and Taro worked to restore the vegetables. Within a month, the ground was productive, and some of the vegetables began to grow again, making it easy for the next team of monks who came on board at the end of September to tend the field. The re-assignments were over, and Taro returned to the kitchen to work in the pantries once again.

Now that the weather was crisper, it would soon be time for some of the monks to return to the city. Four times a year they went, and fall was often a favorite time for them to leave the forest for the day to take part in the ancient ritual of *takuhatsu*. Roshi wanted Taro to have the experience of going into town to exchange sutra blessings for offerings of food or money. He thought it would be good for Taro, as he would gain the understanding of how giver and receiver were one and the same thing.

Throughout the summer, *Gennan* Roshi watched how *Aja* and Taro worked together, and he considered them good partners. Which was why Roshi assigned her to the Stitchery and put her in charge of dressing and preparing Taro for the upcoming *takuhatsu*. Some lay people thought of this as *begging*. It wasn't. The monks were supported by society. The people were given the opportunity to contribute, and in turn, the monks rained blessings down on the villagers. The entire world was seen in this one reciprocal action.

In a private room within the Stitchery, *Aja* considered Taro with a critical eye. "Hmmm, well, let's see what we can do." She had never dressed a cat before, as her own cat Masa would never have tolerated her putting little shirts, hats, or jackets on him. But this was her first assignment as a seamstress, and she would do her best, having never sewn a stitch in her life for anyone other than herself. Taro knew that and loved her for it, no matter what happened.

"Okay. The two most critical pieces are the hat and something to carry donations in, besides the bowl. The monk ahead of you will carry your bowl and place it on the ground in front of you every time the line stops. But I'll sew a satchel you can wear around your neck, in case anyone wants to put money or something else in it. People will offer food in the bowl. I'll inscribe your satchel to identify you as a member of the *Gakiji* Hungry Ghost Temple. That way, people won't think you're just a stray cat following the food trail, hahaha. But when the monks stop, you should sit down so the satchel hangs over your belly. Fair enough?"

"Yes, *Aja*. I promise to do a good job." Taro was so happy to be alone with *Aja* in the sewing room.

"I'm glad you're here in the monastery with us, Taro," *Aja* said, then turned from him quickly to resist the urge to snuggle him. "And now for the tricky part," she said. "The hat. No matter the season, each monk wears an oversized straw hat that's pointed at the top. It has an intentionally very large brim to obstruct the view of the face of any donor. Who that person is or what is given is not important. It's the act of giving that allows both of us to benefit. So. How are we going to construct this?"

Taro was hoping it would take *Aja* a long time to figure this out, but within a few seconds, she took out a tape measure and said, "Let me measure your head and I'll make it work, somehow. I just need to make the brim large enough to cover your face."

"But how will I see anything if the hat is too big?" Taro asked.

"Good question. But really, all you need to see are the feet in front of you. Now back to the kitchen you go, and I'll catch up with you later for a fitting," *Aja* said with a kind laugh and a gentle push off.

Gennan Roshi walked away from the monastery towards the grand, old oak tree, a bowl in each hand. He had another assignment for the birds. As he approached the old oak, it shimmered in greeting and Roshi bowed reverently. Waiting in *zazen*, it took only a minute for the birds to come to him. Chirping happily, they waited for Roshi to speak first.

"Ah! Wonderful! Thank you for coming. Fall is here, and I have a very important assignment I would like to give you."

The birds expressed their excitement. Roshi smiled. After they calmed down, he said, "Some of the monks are preparing to go out for *takuhatsu*. I would like you to go back to the marketplace and find Sachi again. This time, talk to her directly. But only her. Tell her Taro will be coming into the village with some monks next week. When they hear the bells and the monks' chanting, my wish is that Taro's mother will come out and see her son. Taro won't be able to see her, but I would like for her to have the opportunity to see him. Can you manage this, my friends?"

"Of course! Yes! Thank you for this chance to serve you and

Taro. We will leave now and make it happen," Hiroto said on behalf of all.

"Yes! But not before filling yourselves with this seed and cut-up fruit I've brought for you. And I have a bowl of water for you, too." Roshi said as he placed the two bowls on the ground. "Thank you once again. Have a safe flight, and I will speak with you upon your return." Roshi waved to the birds, touched the oak's trunk in a farewell gesture, and turned to go back to the monastery.

Aja walked into the kitchen and held up a straw hat and a satchel for Taro to see. "Look what I have! Come for a fitting. Let's see how it looks."

Taro excused himself to the head cook and quickly followed *Aja* into the sewing room. It was bustling now, monks restoring worn garments and orders being completed for new cushions and robes. As needles, cloth, thread, and scissors went flying, Taro felt grateful he had the pantry as his work assignment. At least it was safe and quiet there.

Aja saw the look on Taro's face and chuckled, "Over here, Taro. There's a private corner for us."

Taro moved quickly and stood still in the corner.

Aja placed the satchel over his neck. "So far, so good. A little wonky, but it's fine," she said, straightening it up. Then she put the hat on his head and burst out laughing. It was several sizes too big and his entire upper body was covered in hat. She tied the strap under his chin and that helped minimally. "Oh, my goodness, Taro. Did you shrink since I measured you?" The green flecks in *Aja's* eyes sparkled. Taro did not care that the hat was too big. Even if it had been too small, she had made it for him and that's all that mattered.

"Well, I do apologize for the oversize, but this is what we've got to work with. I hope you're okay with it," *Aja* said.

Taro nodded his agreement as the hat bobbed forward and back.

When *Aja* removed the hat from Taro's head, she felt the least she could do was give him a good rub behind his ears as a way of making up for the poor fit.

The three birds made good time getting to the village marketplace. Presuming Sachi would be tracking down her family's food there, they would just wait until they saw her.

"So, what's the plan after we see her?" asked Remi as they perched high up on a roof overlooking the village.

"I say we let her grab dinner first, then we stop her on the way home, away from the marketplace," chirped Hiroto.

All agreed this would be the safest scenario. And so they waited, occasionally craning their necks in search of the dark gray furry cat with the imperial green eyes.

Sachi was in no hurry to get to the marketplace that day. She had done a superb job snatching food earlier in the morning, and the family was well fed. But she liked getting out and most of her fun these days came from grabbing people's food right out from underneath their noses. Just to get a reaction.

When Hiroto saw Sachi casually stroll into the marketplace, he whistled and the other two turned their heads, ready to watch the show. And, once again, they were not disappointed. Sachi was a master in the art of food pilfering and was even better than before. She had gotten bolder and took more calculated risks. Like any great sport, it was thrilling to watch.

But, eventually it all came to an end, and Sachi packed up her booty and started to trot off home. The birds hung back. When she turned away from the residential section and started to head out into farmland, the birds took this as their cue and swept down on her. Not so crazily as to frighten her, but with enough persistence that she would be forced to stop.

"Hey!" yelled Sachi, dropping her burlap bag of food on the ground when she cried out. "What are you doing, you crazy birds? Get out of here, or I'll chew your feathers off!"

She jumped up and nipped Genji slightly on his side, scaring the poor little thing half to death. She didn't intend to injure any of the birds. She just wanted them out of her face.

"Sachi, Sachi! We're here to talk to you about Taro. Stop jumping around so we can talk!"

The second she heard Taro's name, Sachi went still and sat down.

The birds were on the excitable side, and it took them a few seconds to calm down.

Finally, Hiroto said, "We live in the forest where Taro is training in the monastery. We were asked by his teacher, *Gennan* Roshi, to tell you that Taro will be coming into the village next week with a group of monks."

"You mean that group of monks that go around chanting and people give them food and things?" Sachi asked. "Taro put food in their bowls once, I remember."

"Yes! And now he will be in the group of monks who are returning to the village. We were asked by his teacher to tell you so that you could let your mother know. His teacher is hoping she will come out when she hears the monks. She will see that Taro is doing well."

"Wait. Mama will have a chance to see Taro next week?" Sachi asked.

"Yes," said Remi. "Taro won't be able to see her, as they have these really big straw hats on, but she will definitely see him. Do you think you could ask your mom to come out? We don't know what day, but you'll hear the bells and chanting."

"Wow. Yeah, I will definitely tell her," Sachi said. "Hey! Thanks for letting me know. And in case there's a next time, all you have to do is fly out a little in front of me. You don't need to flap your wings in my face. One of you especially makes me see red."

The birds looked at her. Hiroto tilted his head.

"That was a joke. Never mind," Sachi said as she picked up her burlap bag and started to head home. Then she stopped and turned. "Hey, bud, sorry about getting you on the side. I didn't mean to hurt you. You okay?"

Genji did a flip in the air as a way of saying *I'm good*, and the three birds flew off in the direction of the forest.

So Taro was coming back with the monks. Sachi wasn't sure how her mother would take the news, but she was excited to tell her. As soon as she got home, she put the food cloth down and said, "Mama, come over here. I have something to tell you." Nori was outside, watching Mika play in the field. For this, Sachi was grateful. She wanted this to be a private conversation, because she didn't know how her mother would react to the news.

Reiko approached her daughter and gave her a loving lick on the top of her head.

Then Sachi said, "Mama, I've been told to tell you that Taro is coming into town next week with the forest monks. Let's take a walk out when he comes and see him, even though he won't be able to see us. What do you think?"

"Taro? Here? Next week?" was all Reiko could say. She was flabbergasted and her heart started to pound. No one had spoken of Taro to her since his departure. She never thought anyone would speak his name out loud again. Much less be told he was coming back to the village.

"Yes, Mama. You don't have to do anything. In fact, you won't even be able to say anything to him, and he won't see you. Just watch him as he walks with the rest of the monks. That's all."

Reiko felt a most tender longing for her son, but she also felt nervous at the thought of being in his presence again. She had been so harsh and angry when he'd left. Turning from Sachi, she walked over to the gray pouch on top of the box in the corner and touched it. Even from where she stood, she could smell the powdered incense that had magically shown up at their home's entrance several months ago. She breathed deeply and let her mind drift to wherever it wanted to go.

For Taro, 3:00 a.m. was early, but he was so excited to go out for *takuhatsu*, he had not slept well anyway. For the past week, he had practiced walking in his oversized hat and felt prepared for the day.

Dressed in traditional attire, the monks' robes were rolled up and secured at the waist to expose white cloth leggings, but the conventional grass sandals had long been given over to white sneakers, which were infinitely more practical and comfortable. The monks would put the hats on once they hit the outskirts of the village. Until then, the walk through the forest was invigorating, as the lead monks set a fast pace.

Taro loved moving through the forest this way. He breathed in deeply and smelled the scents from the plants and flowers growing on the floor of the forest. Creatures awakened, going about their business of foraging for food. Those who were in the path of the monks moved out of the way and acknowledged them with happy morning sounds. The monks all smiled, waved, and kept moving forward. It was going to be a lovely day.

Within the hour, the group could see the outline of the village, and many had already started to don their hats in preparation for the official alms-giving practice.

Two senior monks holding hand bells were responsible for Taro's group. One senior led, the other brought up the rear. They ventured forth in single file to the marketplace, heading toward a row of storefronts in a commercial area. The novitiates formed the middle of the group, two of whom carried wooden staffs with three rings atop that jingled when they walked. The third was Taro. He had been told to just follow the feet in front of him and not worry about carrying a wooden staff.

After all his enthusiastic rehearsal, Taro realized too late that the one piece he had not practiced was walking in his very large hat as part of a group. If he got too close to the junior monk in front of him, he couldn't see his feet, bumped into him, and the hat started to move in circles around his head. If he stayed too far back, the senior monk behind him began to stutter step and Taro felt the accidental kick of a foot, which also sent the hat spinning around his head. He needed to keep pace with the rhythm of the monks' walk. So maybe the kick wasn't so accidental after all. All he knew was he didn't want to be the reason the Fall *takuhatsu* was a bumbling failure and a joke to the community or to *Gakiji*.

Once in the village, each monk, within his or her own time, rhythm, and capacity, chanted a deep-bellied, prolonged "*Hōoooo* . . ." meaning the rain of the teachings. It was a vibrant, rich, and unmistakable sound, especially when accompanied by the tinkle of the bells. The monks were offering a pouring out of teachings and blessings onto anyone who, in exchange, would reciprocate with food, valuables, or money. The ringing of the hand bells and the bells atop the staffs announced the monks' arrival.

Reiko and Sachi heard the bells and the chanting far in the distance. Sachi looked at her mother with the question she did not have to ask. Reiko was nervous but knew she would never forgive herself if she didn't get out there to see Taro. This was something she owed him and wanted for herself as well. She picked up Sachi's burlap bag with several red potatoes in it and walked outside toward Nori. Mika was bunny kicking a twig. "Nori," her mother said, "I'm leaving for a little while. Are you okay watching Mika on your own?"

"Of course, Mama. Take your time. Everything is fine."

Reiko and Sachi briskly ran in the direction of the sounds, positioning themselves well ahead of where the monks were expected to walk. People went up to the monks and placed gifts of food in their bowls, and money and valuables in their satchels. With each offering, the monks chanted blessings and scripture back onto the people.

Even from a distance, Reiko noticed the gap between two monks towards the end of the line and wondered if Taro was the reason for that. As the line came closer, she did, indeed, see Taro. To be clear, she saw his paws and his tail. His head and most of his body were covered by an enormous straw hat that moved slightly from side to side. The monks reached Reiko, Sachi, and the people they stood among. They stopped and turned to face the group. Taro sat down, almost in front of his mother. His hat, wobbling from side to side, nearly came down to the ground. Reiko's nerves vanished completely. The hat looked so silly. Several of the villagers commented when they realized a cat was in line with the monks.

"Oh my goodness, it's a cat. How adorable!"

"Wow! What a fantastic cat!"

"What? No way. Move over. Let me see."

"I didn't know cats could be monks. Hey, kids! Come over here and look at this."

"What a lucky Temple!"

When Reiko heard the comments of the villagers, she was filled with pride. The monk next to Taro bent down and placed a bowl in front of him. The villagers made their contributions, and Reiko stepped forward with her burlap bag. The monks acknowledged their appreciation with their chants and blessings.

Then the monk picked up Taro's bowl and all together they turned and started walking farther down the street, bells tinkling and jingling. *"Hōoooo . . ."*

Reiko was silent on the way home, but Sachi could not stop talking. "Wow, that was crazy! Taro looked great, don't you think? Well, his paws and tail looked good. Maybe he's grown a little, too. Hey, Mama, what did you think?"

Reiko didn't want to think or talk. She wanted to be with her memory of Taro, silly straw hat and all. It had been a precious moment, and she wanted to hold onto it for as long as she could without any distractions.

"Sachi, go ahead of me and find Nori and Mika. Or maybe get them a treat in the marketplace. Just go now."

Sachi took the hint. She ran up ahead towards their home in search of her sisters to tell them what had just happened before she went to get them something special.

The day was fun for Taro, even if he had only seen the heels of the monk in front of him. People had put money in his satchel and, as far as he knew, had even dropped food donations in his bowl. He was excited to get back to the monastery to add what he had to the monks' pile that was poured out onto a table in the kitchen. He had done his part for the fall *takuhatsu,* grateful for the opportunity to give back to the community and the monastery.

One by one, the monks approached the table in the kitchen. Satchels were emptied first, and mostly money rolled onto the table, but some satchels held a few rings and there were three gold bracelets. Then the monks' bowls were emptied of all food. This food would be taken by the head cook and included in upcoming meals. Each monk went in order, adding to the assortment of valuables and food on the table. When it was Taro's turn, the monk who had been carrying Taro's bowl tipped it over, and out fell four red potatoes, an onion, six little crab apples, a wrapped-up piece of fish, and one shiny black button studded with rhinestones.

CHAPTER Fourteen

THE BUTTON ROLLED out of Taro's bowl and landed in front of him. He immediately sucked in his breath and uttered a low cry. The monks gathered around the table were concerned and started moving in to comfort him. A button to them was a child's innocent offering, not the source of anguish.

But this was no child who had placed the shiny button in Taro's bowl. His mother had done it. And this one trinket, this button with the rhinestones, represented a world of value, importance, and meaning to Taro. This button meant his mother had acknowledged him and was willing to see him as he meant himself to be seen.

And so he protected the button as one would a newborn. He held it, licked it, and did not let others stare at it for too long. Certainly, he never allowed anyone to pick it up or breathe on it. He valued this precious object because it said to Taro that his mother still loved him. And he was not willing to ever let that go again.

He would have liked the button to have been with him at all times, but Taro had no pockets. So he kept it under his pillow in the room he shared with several other monks. Every morning upon waking, he picked up the button, licked it, and said, "Good morning, Mama. My life is good because of you. I love you. Thank you." Before he went to sleep, he would pick up the button again, hold it, purr into it, and say, "Mama, I know how hard it was for you to let me go, but my life is good and I love you. Thank you. Good night, Mama." These prayers of Taro's became a ritual, and he couldn't start his day or go to sleep until he acknowledged his mother in this way.

Ratzitzu lurked in the corner and listened to Taro saying the same thing over and over. *What an obnoxious little mama's boy! Blah, blah, good morning. Blah, blah, and goodnight. I love you, Mama. UGH!* He thought about taking that stupid button and burying it deep in the ground somewhere. But then he knew Taro would go off like a rocket and somehow, some way, now that *Gennan* Roshi knew he was there, the accusing finger would point directly at Ratzitzu. And then maybe someone from Taro's dumbass fan club of monks would come after him with a rake or a shovel to do him in. No, no. He would figure out another way to get back at this irritating fool he hated so much.

Ratzitzu knew he could never say, "Hey Mom, thanks for loving me enough." What mother? She didn't even know who he was. And come to think of it, he didn't know who she was, either. Or his thousands of siblings. Some family. And so, every single night now, Ratzitzu allowed a few indulgent moments to feel sorry for himself and his poor, pitiful little life. He didn't love anyone and no one loved him. *Wah-wah.*

Taro's connection with his mother gave him a quiet joy. He was at peace. And what easily flowed from this was love and compassion for others.

As part of his duties in the kitchen, Taro continued to be responsible for keeping the pantries clean. He dusted shelves, rotated cans and bags, kept the baskets of fruits and vegetables clean, and of course swept the floors several times a day. He knew he had a love-hate relationship with the turds in the corner. But there were so many every day, and he knew now that Ratzitzu was the one who made this mess.

Taro had hoped that the rat would go away after their confrontation in the forest, but the rat was sticking like fly paper. Taro never knew when or where the bully would show up again. Clearly, Ratzitzu had started the wreckage of the vegetable garden as well.

The button changed everything, though. Taro no longer cared to give any mental energy to Ratzitzu or his turds in the corner. They were there. His job was to sweep them up and deposit them in a proper place outside. That was it.

As Taro walked outside, carrying the dustpan filled with the rat evidence, Momo and her white tuft of hair blowing in the wind ran up to him. "Hi, Taro, hi! Hi!" she said. "What are you doing? What's up?"

Taro smiled at the sweet little field mouse, feeling so grateful he hadn't killed her. "I'm cleaning up a mess from the pantry corner. Look," he said as he showed her the dustpan.

"Oh. That's probably from that rat, you know. . .what's his name?" Momo asked.

"Ratzitzu."

Momo put her little paw to her mouth to cover a giggle. "Well, whatever. He needs to learn where to go outside like the rest of us. I've run into him before, you know."

"No. Where?"

"He was digging up to the pantry entrance. We had a few words. He was defensive and all puffed up, but I thought he had, ummm, potential, I guess you could say. Although now I'm thinking he should learn some manners first. You know. Some decorum."

"You have a crush on him," Taro teased.

"What? Oh my goodness, Taro, no. No! No, no, no, no, no. What? No!" Momo said as she twirled her hair sprout tighter and tighter around her paw.

Taro burst out laughing. "Well, then, maybe you can coach him along on the ways of the forest world."

"His teeth look better, don't you think?" Momo asked eagerly, talking right over Taro.

"You know, honestly, I hadn't . . . um . . . uh, why, yes! Now that you mention it, yes! His teeth do look better. Absolutely," Taro said with a smile.

Before returning to the kitchen, he said, "You know, Momo, maybe you're just the one to teach that rat those manners. What do you think?"

Momo beamed up at Taro. "Me? Really? You think so? Well, that's not such a bad idea." This was exactly what she wanted to hear. In Momo's mind, Taro had just given her permission to approach the rat again. "Yes! I'll go see him. Thank you, Taro! Thank you! I have to go now!" And with that, Momo scurried off into the woods, a plan forming in her little brain.

The days grew shorter and the nights even colder each week. Dark, cold nights always made *Gennan* Roshi hungrier than usual. The head cook was brilliant at keeping the priests' bodies nourished, but Roshi usually craved more than the 5:00 p.m. bowl of soup and piece of bread. He wasn't a big person. In fact, he was lean and wiry. But when those munchies came up, he acknowledged them and always left his room and made his way back to the kitchen.

As Roshi walked from his room to the kitchen, he passed by the *zendo*. Except during intensive periods of training such as *sesshin*, most monks slept peacefully in their rooms after the last period of *zazen*, which ended at 9:00 p.m. And they did not re-enter the *zendo* again until 4:00 a.m. the following morning. Despite that, Roshi always made it a point to look in the direction of the *zendo* on his way to the kitchen. He never knew who or what he would find there during these late-night hours.

Tonight, Roshi saw nothing. He made his way into the pantry that Taro kept so clean, grabbed some fruit and nuts, and went back to his room. There was no need to tip-toe. Nothing to manage or be aware of. No one to disturb.

Ratzitzu waited for Roshi to leave before he came out into the kitchen from underneath the sink.

He needed to get the lay of the kitchen, as he had with the vegetable garden, in case the kitchen was where he would make his final strike on Taro. He wanted to study where the shelves were, the counters, where the pantries were in relation to the sinks, how high the sinks were, where the cauldrons were, and if the fires were somehow lit all night. They weren't. He wanted to know where the cooks kept their knives, what types of knives there were, and the weight of each. Slicing, utility, paring, vegetable, butcher – these were different types of knives, and the kitchen was stocked with various sizes of each. He had to be as familiar with these as he was with the layout of the kitchen. Ratzitzu wanted no surprises and could afford no mistakes.

Rohatsu

The eighth day of the twelfth month. December 8. This was recognized as Buddha's Enlightenment and, as with many Zen Buddhist Temples, was observed on the last day of a week-long *sesshin*. Every year at *Gakiji*, the *Rohatsu Sesshin* began its intensive training on the evening of December 1.

Preparations were being made and were especially intensified with the kitchen staff and *Gennan* Roshi. The other monks maintained their daily rituals, showed up to the *zendo* on time, inquired into their *kōans*, fulfilled their work practice duties, and kept going.

In the kitchen, Taro made sure the shelves were stocked appropriately, that fruits and vegetables were fresh and would make it through eight days when the countdown began. He had to know which foods would perish faster than others so that he offered the right ones at the right times. If he calculated incorrectly, food would be wasted. And he had had enough of wasted food.

Although Roshi did a significant amount of teaching in individual sessions during *dokusan,* he leveraged his message through dharma talks. Just as *Ekō* Roshi's dharma talk highlighted Ratzitzu's pride and arrogance, *Gennan* Roshi also used the public arena to expose sticking points and resistances in his monks. Sometimes this was done individually, other times collectively. Teaching moments were organic and impossible to plan. But there was always a reason for them and opportunities were endless during *sesshin*.

Roshi's dharma talks were a formal affair. Everyone sat motionless in a *zazen* posture and focused on Roshi's words with their eyes lowered. There was no talking, no slouching, and no interaction among the monks during this time.

After a week of intensive training, practice, and inquiry, Roshi prepared his dharma talk for the final evening of the *Rohatsu Sesshin* to address the collective. Enlightenment was close for some, but elusive for most. There was no time to waste.

He began his talk in the usual manner. "Well, good evening, everyone," he said as he scanned the group of monks, none of whom looked up at him. "We are going into the final night of *Rohatsu* and most of you are still holding on. Some of you may be close to a breakthrough, but can't quite get there because you're grasping. You're holding on to something. And it's costing you. Why can't you let go? You'll never get to the purpose of *sesshin,* you'll never penetrate your *kōans* to reach the enlightenment you say you want unless you let go. Stop wasting your time! What are you hanging on to? What is it you cherish most?"

Taro squirmed in his seat, thinking about his button.

Roshi continued, "You're all like greedy monkeys up in the trees! Impossible to catch. But hunters finally learned how to capture these monkeys. Do you know how? They take a coconut, make a small hole in it, and hollow it out, removing all the meat. Then they stick a treat, like a piece of candy, in the bottom of the coconut, and scatter the coconuts on the ground. The monkey smells whatever the treat is, comes down out of the tree, and sticks his hand in the coconut to grab the candy. The hunters know the monkey can't get his hand out of the coconut unless he lets go of the treat. If the monkey does let go, he can easily get his hand out through the hole and be free. All the monkey has to do is let go of the treat and his hand would come right out. But he won't let go. It's about grasping and hanging on. The monkey is so greedy, so narrow-minded and fixated on that treat, he'd rather die than let it go. And the hunters know this about the monkey. So when the monkey is trying to get his hand out of the coconut without letting go of the treat, the hunters cast a net. And that is the end of the monkey."

There was some rustling of fabric. Taro stole a quick sideways glance and noticed that several monks seated nearby looked uncomfortable.

Gennan Roshi continued, "Each of you is holding on to something. It could be an idea, a point of view. For some of you, it's an object. For some, it's another person. For others, it's a feeling. Most of you are feeling self-pity. But it's costing you. How long are you willing to hold on? It's time to let go! That treat, that candy, could be your hatred for someone else. Some of you are hanging onto grudges or resentments. Will you hang onto your treasured animosity, your outrage, until it kills you? In your grasping and desire to kill the other, the one you kill is you! Blame! There is no freedom in this!" he said as he pounded the podium.

Roshi scanned the room carefully and noted the tension. Good. "The cause of your suffering is grasping and holding onto ideas, points of view, beliefs, notions that you put ahead of everything else. One finger points out, three fingers point back!" Roshi said as he jabbed his finger out into the unseeing group of monks. He knew they could all feel it, though. "This is no different than what the Buddha was tempted with and had to confront. All his cherished ideas, beliefs, feelings when he was sitting under the Bodhi tree. He had to drop them all away before he could achieve enlightenment!"

Taro was so uncomfortable. Roshi was right. Taro vowed to release his greedy hold over the button and let others look at it and touch it if they wanted to.

Gennan Roshi continued, "The coconut and that stupid monkey take in the totality of your entire being. This is it! This is the last night of *Rōhatsu*. Do you want your freedom? Listen to the Evening Gatha tonight and remember the words. This is not a lullaby to put you to sleep. It is chanted to **wake you up!** Do you want to penetrate your *kōan* and achieve enlightenment? Then stop grasping! **Let go!"**

And with one final fist pounding on the podium, *Gennan* Roshi's dharma talk concluded.

Let me respectfully remind you
Life and death are of supreme importance
Time swiftly passes by and opportunity is lost
Each of us must strive to awaken
Awaken! Take heed!
Do not squander your life
~ *Evening Gatha* ~

Ratzitzu heard Roshi's talk from the safety of another room near the *zendo. Ho hum yeah, yeah. Monkey treat, big fist in coconut. Got it, Gennan. Why can't you understand just one basic principle? It's not rocket science. I will have no need to grasp once Taro is out of the picture. How complicated is that? Get rid of the problem. Buh-bye. Freedom!* No. More than ever, Ratzitzu's plan needed to stay in place. He was done with Taro. He just needed for the *sesshin* to be over with.

For the week following *Rohatsu*, Taro slept fitfully, often waking and thinking about how much he craved his button while knowing he needed to release his grasp on it. Since Roshi's dharma talk, he wanted to put the button away in a secure place and stop thinking about it so much. But that wouldn't mean he would stop thinking about his mother. Just the symbol of her. The button. That's all he wanted. Yet, the thought of finding a safe place that wasn't that far away invaded his sleep and kept waking him up. And from there, he would stretch, yawn, scratch, and lick.

Finally several of the monks, bothered by Taro's untimely ritual, yelled out, "Stop! Be quiet! Get out and go sit or something!" inferring he should get out of the bedroom, go sit in the *zendo,* and leave them in peace.

Taro thought it was good advice, and he was sorry he had angered the monks by waking them. He loved sitting, and the smell of the incense always grounded him in a center point of peace and stability.

From a corner in Taro's communal bedroom, Ratzitzu watched Taro leave and head out. Ratzitzu thought that maybe the big baby would go stuff himself in the kitchen because his puddy tat feelings had been hurt. Or maybe he'd take the hint and go sit in the *zendo*. Either would do for Ratzitzu. If no one else was in the *zendo,* Ratzitzu would make his move there tonight. Hurrying to the kitchen ahead of Taro, Ratzitzu pulled a knife out from the drawer and waited to see which way Taro went.

Ratzitzu had studied the kitchen well and knew it like the

back of his paw. But he was also prepared to attack Taro in the *zendo*. The eight-inch paring knife he had chosen was the sharpest one in the kitchen's drawer that was manageable. It was big for Ratzitzu, but he had been practicing with it for nearly a week and felt he had the right balance on it, knew exactly where to hold it so the blade would have its deadliest angle. It was a lethal weapon, and Ratzitzu was ready. He went over scenarios in his head, how he would attack if Taro went one way, or what he would do if the dumb cat went in the other direction. Ratzitzu knew he had the element of surprise on his side.

An impatient Ratzitzu waited. Finally, he saw Taro approach and turn away from the kitchen. Show time!

Taro entered the *zendo*, bowed at the threshold, and went directly to the altar. He lit the candle, then lit a long stick of incense from the candle flame and placed it in the bowl in the center of the altar. He bowed as he left the altar, went to his seat, and bowed again. Sitting in traditional *zazen* style, Taro turned on his cushion to face the wall. The silence, the ambient light from the candle flame, and the whisper of smoke from the incense were perfect for his solitary sitting. From there, Taro centered himself, gazed at the wall, and began his *zazen*.

Ratzitzu's heart beat so rapidly, he struggled to think over the thudding. He took a few deep breaths. Then, with the knife gripped in both paws and extended before him, he made his way to the *zendo*.

As he approached the threshold, Ratzitzu stopped and looked around. He heard and saw nothing. He peeked in and saw Taro sitting alone, his back to him. *Yes! My great karma!* Since Taro was in a seated posture, Ratzitzu thought a plunge down into Taro's back would do the trick.

Ratzitzu crossed the threshold and crept slowly up behind Taro, his paws held high, the knife pointed slightly downward. Closer and closer. Once Ratzitzu plunged the knife deep into Taro, he would be free.

Taro sensed it first before he saw out of the corner of his eye a shadowy movement on the wall. Without turning his head, he saw an elongated body, rounded ears, pointy snout, and a thin tail sticking up. The paws were up high, holding what looked like a long knife. Faster, and then faster and faster, the shadow grew as it moved towards Taro.

A heartbeat before Taro saw the looming shadow of Ratzitzu's body arch back slightly and his paws rise higher, Taro did a sharp, deep lean to the left and the knife sliced by him and rammed into the wall. Momentum carried Ratzitzu forward. His belly slammed into the knife's handle, punching him backward. His body did a half spin on the polished wooden floor, and he found himself sprawled out on his back in front of Taro.

Taro looked down. "You should be more careful. You could cut yourself with that thing." He motioned to the cushion next to him. "Have a seat."

Ratzitzu immediately pulled himself up, humiliated that all his planning had ended in such dismal failure. He spewed out a final, "I hate you, Taro!" The knife fell out of the wall and clattered onto the floor.

Ratzitzu felt like a deflated balloon that had just emitted its final puff of air. Taro had known Ratzitzu was coming. Why didn't he fight back? Then Ratzitzu could have justified any harm that he inflicted on Taro. Even his death. But no. That's not the move Taro made. Instead, he extended an open paw to an empty seat.

Taro turned halfway around on his cushion to face Ratzitzu and offered the knife back to him. "Here. You forgot something."

Ratzitzu's hatred turned to shame. The sheer expansiveness of Taro's invitation was beyond any show of mercy or acceptance Ratzitzu had ever experienced. He stared up at Taro. Everything Ratzitzu had taken for granted in his life - his bitter resentment, jealousy, alienation – began to crack and shift. This hell realm he had been living in was shattered with one simple gesture. Taro's lifted paw motioning for him to take the empty seat next to him.

Ratzitzu was so powerfully overcome with the realization of what he had almost done to Taro, he started to weep.

"Come on, Ratzitzu. Let's sit together," Taro said.

Ratzitzu took the knife from Taro, walked over to the cushion next to him and laid the knife down. Then he climbed up onto the cushion and sat down facing the wall.

Taro kept his eyes lowered on the wall. "Let's bow to our mutual teacher."

And a cat and a rat, sitting next to each other in a *zendo* in the early morning hours, bowed to the wall together.

Gennan Roshi was making another midnight run to the kitchen when he heard a shout then a clank from the *zendo*. Fearing the candle holder had somehow fallen off the altar and landed on someone, he poked his head in the semi-darkened entrance and was stunned to see Ratzitzu on his back, staring up at Taro. There was a kitchen knife on the floor. Roshi was prepared to jump in, but he knew from decades of training that, as he saw and felt no immediate danger, he should not intervene. He strained to hear what was being said between the two.

As the story unfolded, Roshi sucked in his breath. The rat hated Taro so much, he had tried to kill him! But Taro just offered the rat a seat. Roshi felt his throat get scratchy and his eyes water as he thought what life would be like without Taro. An ache came over him, but he forced himself to shake it off and listen.

He saw Taro extend the knife to Ratzitzu.

Roshi watched closely.

There! There it was! That's what Roshi was looking for. The shift on Ratzitzu's face. Roshi knew instantly that Taro understood what he was doing.

From the shadows, Roshi made a standing bow to the altar in deep appreciation to the Ancestors for their teachings of such profound wisdom and intelligence. Enlightenment was possible for anyone. Taro had proven it, using grace and skill in a life and death moment. This was the equanimity that *Gennan* Roshi needed to see before he could entrust anyone to carry on his lineage.

Now, Roshi knew who would be next in line for ordination.

CHAPTER *Fifteen*

GENNAN ROSHI always looked out several generations ahead. It was one thing to know the plans for the coming week, or what needed to be taken care of by the end of the month. But the dharma, the Buddha's teaching, was a sacred gift that had been passed down from teacher to student for thousands of years. It was Roshi's responsibility to ensure that whoever he entrusted as a vessel to hold these teachings had earned the right and the privilege to become a monk in his lineage and would carry the dharma out into the world for future generations.

In May, *Gennan* Roshi would officiate the ordination ceremony known as *tokudo*, and install Taro in the *Gakiji* Hungry Ghost Temple as its newest Zen Buddhist monk.

Momo had to get up her nerve before revisiting Ratzitzu. But it was with Taro's blessing after all. And it was in thinking she might help Ratzitzu adjust to life in the forest, that she made her way along Ratzitzu's tunnel. Then she heard some shuffling behind her. Being high-strung anyway, she overreacted and jumped up off the ground, hitting her head on the top of the low tunnel ceiling.

Ratzitzu looked at her without expression. "It's a good thing you're wearing that helmet on your head for protection."

Momo immediately became flustered. "Why, look who's here!" she said. "How nice of you to come. Please, come in." Oh, no. That was backwards. No, no, no! Had she just said that?

Ratzitzu, unschooled in any response other than hatred, outrage, or sarcasm, rolled his eyes. "I live here. This is my tunnel. What's wrong with you?"

Frequently feeling there was something wrong with her, Momo cast her eyes downward, embarrassed. "I, I, I'm sorry. A silly mistake. I'm sorry. Excuse me. I didn't mean . . . I'll be leaving now," she stuttered as she tried to make her way around the rat.

Ratzitzu did not give her the space to do that. Instead, he studied her for a long second. And then with no thought given to what he would do next, he reached out and touched her tuft of hair. "I must have scared you so badly, your hair turned white."

Momo's giggles, released upon the sheer build-up of anxiety, became so contagious, Ratzitzu joined in right along with her and genuinely laughed for the first time in his life.

Shortly after *Gennan* Roshi had decided upon the ordination, he called Taro into his *dokusan* room and motioned for him to take a seat.

"Taro," he began, "you've proven yourself to be a loyal student. You have embodied the dharma in ways that are mature and wise for the time you have been here. I saw your interaction with Ratzitzu the night he tried to kill you."

"You saw that?"

Roshi nodded. "I made a conscious decision not to intervene, as I felt no imminent threat by the time I saw you. I wanted to see what you would do. Although I knew it was potentially risky, I had faith in you."

"You had faith in me?" Taro repeated as he flashed back on that night and the damage Ratzitzu's knife had done to the wall, a big chunk of which had fallen out.

Roshi nodded. "I did. And now your next step is to continue your training and practice as a Zen Buddhist monk. I was thinking springtime under the cherry trees would be beautiful for your ordination. As we get closer, the birds will invite your family and guide them to the ceremony."

Taro remembered his Entering Ceremony. There was a moment of confusion, because Taro had been told indirectly that the Entering Ceremony was for him when *Daishin* originally announced it to the head cook. But now, Roshi was personally telling him that he would become a monk. And with that intimate announcement, so special to Taro, he bowed deeply to *Gennan* Roshi. The vision that Taro had held for himself for such a long time, now possessed shape and substance. Ordination in the spring. And his family would be invited to come, too.

The logistics involved in the making of a monk would be different with Taro, and *Gennan* Roshi called *Aja* in for assistance.

Roshi smiled as *Aja* walked into his *dokusan* room. He motioned for her to sit down. "Welcome!" he said. "I need some help. In five months, in late May, when the cherry blossoms are in full bloom, I will install Taro as our newest monk."

Aja shot her arms up in the air. The wide, long sleeves from her robes fluttered down to her shoulders. "Woo hoo, Roshi! That's fantastic!" She started to high-five him, but stopped, wondering if he even knew what that meant. Best to just return her hands to her lap.

Roshi smiled at *Aja's* exuberance. That's what he loved about the young ones. "Yes. And I'm going to need your help. Within these next five months, I'd like you to make him a complete set of robes, a jacket, and of course the black *rakusu*. Please bring them to me when you've finished, so I can ink the back of the *rakusu*. Oh, and be sure to give Taro as many details of the ordination ceremony as you can think of."

Aja beamed at Roshi as she bowed respectfully to him. She was thrilled to be offered the chance to work with Taro again. She trusted that her sewing skills had advanced and were now up to the task.

Taro was busy in the kitchen as usual, and he didn't see *Aja* make her way back to the pantry area.

"Taro, oh Taro, look who's here!" she said softly in a singsongy voice.

He immediately turned, ran up to her and jumped into her arms, purring on her face.

Aja laughed as she bent down and gently put him back on the ground, self-consciously looking around to make sure no one had seen that. "Guess why I'm here. Never mind. I'll tell you. I'm going to get you ready for your *tokudo*. We have some garments we need to make, so see if you can take some time from the kitchen so we can get started. I'll wait at the door."

Within less than a minute, Taro raced across the floor. He and *Aja* entered the Stitchery, then went into a private room with a cutting table on the side wall.

"So, here's what we're going to do, Taro," *Aja* said as she brought out a measuring tape, bolts of black and white fabric, straight pins, and a box. "The robes that monks wear . . . like mine? I will make a set for you. And Roshi said to make you a jacket, too. This is something you might wear a lot. They're kind of snappy looking. Look! Over there. See that monk with the purple fabric in his hand? He has on a jacket. It's called a *samue*."

"It will be strange wearing clothing," Taro said.

"You can do it! And this black fabric will look great against your orange fur. Anyway, it crisscrosses in the front, so we'll have to figure out how to keep the belt tied. Then you'll look like you're ready for some taekwondo. Heeyah!!" *Aja* said as she faked a high karate chop through the air.

Taro burst out laughing. *Aja* was so silly and free. But then she became serious again as she carefully took out a model *rakusu* from the box, unfolded it, and laid it flat on the table.

"Taro, look at this. This is a *rakusu* and it represents a small version of the monk's robe, or *kesa*. I'm going to alter one to fit you. You wear it around your neck like this." She placed it around Taro's neck, pinching it up in back to keep it from dragging. Of course, it was still way too big, but he began to get the idea. "It's a sacred garment that you'll want to respect and protect at all times after Roshi officially gives it to you during the ordination ceremony."

Taro brought one paw up to the center of the *rakusu*. "Does this mean anything?" indicating the staggered, brick-like pattern in the center.

"Yes, it's been said it represents the pattern of rows in the rice fields the Buddha saw when he walked around the countryside. So, for thousands of years now, this pattern has been sewn on the *kesas* and *rakusus* of Buddhists.

"Also, Taro," *Aja* continued as she turned the garment over, "you'll notice on this model *rakusu* that the back is just plain white. On this blank side, Roshi will ink your dharma name, stamp it with the *Gakiji* seal, date the ceremony, and write whatever he wishes. Look at mine." She turned hers over for Taro to see.

"A dharma name? I'm going to be given a dharma name? What does that mean, *Aja*?"

"Well," *Aja* said, "all of us are given a dharma name when we're ordained. It's a name Roshi creates that he believes represents the parts of us that we have a bigger potential to live into.

They are very large names and become the vision he holds for us as we move forward in our training and practice with our lives."

"Wait. You mean your name isn't really *Aja*?"

She laughed. "When I was born, my parents named me Sumi. When I came here to train with *Gennan* Roshi and received ordination a few years ago, he presented me with the dharma name *Aja*. I always think of myself as *Aja* now, even though my birth name is Sumi."

Taro hesitated for a moment then said, "*Aja*, can I ask you a question?"

"Of course! Anything."

"Why did you come to the monastery to train with Roshi?"

Aja looked at Taro. Such an innocent question, yet she knew enough about his past to know this was not a superficial question and that he deserved a thoughtful answer. Finally, she said, "For a long time, before I met Roshi, I felt sort of hollow and empty inside. My life had no substance. I was just going through some motions my parents expected of me. I wanted to live a meaningful life in service, but I really didn't know what that meant or what it would look like. I just knew I had outgrown my former, material life."

"Did your parents support your decision to come here?"

"No, they didn't. At least not at first. I remember before I came here, they kept buying me things like expensive trips, or thinking clothes, or shoes, even a car would make me happy.

"But it didn't?"

"No, it made things worse. The more they gave me, the sadder I felt. My parents were trying but they didn't understand. I wanted a life that I couldn't articulate for them or for myself at the time. But I knew there was a right path for me somewhere."

"So what happened, *Aja*?"

"Well, I found out about *Gakiji*, met with Roshi, and when I was accepted, I surrendered to the practice and I guess you could say the lights of the training led me home. Training with

Roshi fulfills me every day. I don't know if you understand that, but . . ."

Taro looked at his friend and absolutely knew what she was talking about. It wasn't an exact blueprint of his life, but the major pieces were there.

"Thank you. And yes, I do understand. What does the name *Aja* mean?" Taro asked.

"Roshi saw me as someone who had the qualities of creation and protection, and the possibility to be someone who used these qualities to reduce suffering in the world. I don't have a model for it, so I don't know how to reduce suffering or even explain it. I *be* it, I guess you could say."

"That's beautiful! So after my *tokudo*, you're going to call me something else, too?" Taro asked.

"Yes! Everyone here will call you by your new dharma name."

"Do you know what it is?"

Aja couldn't contain herself and bubbled over in laughter. "No, of course not! But trust me, Roshi gives this part of the *tokudo* his gravest consideration. Soon you'll only see yourself as your dharma name. It's a very personal, one-of-a-kind gift that Roshi will create for you and present during your ceremony."

When Momo and Ratzitzu finally stopped laughing, Momo said, "Why don't you come out, and I'll introduce you to my friends? I can show you the best places to find things to eat, where the biggest piles of acorns are that are thrown off by the oak tree, great places to live, the best forest bathrooms, you know . . . come with me."

Ratzitzu knew exactly what that bathroom comment meant. But, meeting other animals right now? "No. There's been enough excitement for one day. You need to go home and calm yourself down."

For all her excitability, Momo could still be levelheaded. Hearing Ratzitzu's resistance, she conceded. "Okay. Then let's just go to the opening of your tunnel and look out at the forest. It should be quiet. Come on. Follow me!" She scooted around him and hoped he would catch up with her at the tunnel's entrance.

He did. And there they stayed. Two field creatures peeking out the entryway, gnawing on sticks together until the sun went down several hours later.

About a month after *Gennan* Roshi spoke with Taro about his ordination, he summoned the birds to him again. Waiting under the cluster of cherry trees, the birds quickly came, fluttering their wings in excitement. "We're here, Roshi. All in and at your service."

Roshi always smiled when he saw these beautiful birds. "Ah! Lovely! Here. Have some dried fruit while I ask for your assistance." Roshi presented the birds with a plateful of chopped up dried apricots and raisins.

The birds happily chirped and ate while Roshi continued, "Within another month or two, I plan on having an ordination ceremony for Taro right here under these cherry trees."

The birds stopped eating, looked up simultaneously, then began to excitedly tweet and flap over one another while dried fruit flipped off the plate in all directions. "We love that, Roshi! It will be wonderful!"

Gennan Roshi was pleased. He felt the birds were always a good barometer of the emotional well-being of the creatures in the forest. He continued. "I'd like you to check in again on Taro's family. Observe them from a distance. No talking just yet. I want to make sure everyone is doing well now that another year has passed. There's no date yet, but when I have one, I'll ask you to invite the family to follow you back to *Gakiji* for the ceremony."

"We're as good as gone, Roshi. See you soon, and thanks, we

loved the fruit!" And the three birds flew off in the direction of the village marketplace.

Sachi had been deeply affected by Taro and the other monks when they passed through the village so many months ago. There was something about the people joyfully giving food and money to the monks, who in turn showered them with the dharma, chants, and blessings of goodwill and hope. It seemed like such a powerful way to keep everyone engaged, giving the best of what each had. To give and receive and receive and give. On and on like a perfect circle, a wheel that just rolled down the street, never ending. Everyone felt fulfilled and walked away happier for it.

I could do something like that, Sachi thought. *I don't have to be a monk to contribute to someone else. I have a gift that I could share.* And she set about figuring out what that would look like.

The birds whooped and hollered as they made their way back once again to the marketplace. They would just observe Sachi for a while, follow her home, check in from a distance on all the sisters and mama cat, and then report back to Roshi. An easy assignment for them.

It was a beautiful day, unseasonably warm for the end of March. The birds were sunning themselves on a rooftop when Sachi sauntered into their view. "Heads up. She's here," whistled Hiroto.

The three birds watched as Sachi slowly strolled through the marketplace. To an untrained eye, she looked like any cat who was casually walking around with nothing in particular on her mind. But the birds knew she was setting up the coordinates for her next attack. Thirty seconds later, a diner bent down to pick up her fallen napkin. In one fluid movement, Sachi swooped in and ran off with the chicken breast on her plate, leaving behind scattered Brussels sprouts rolling on the tablecloth when the unfortunate diner sat back up again.

And on and on this magical show went for almost an hour. Sachi's sack was so full by the time she left the marketplace, Remi said, "Geez, I wonder if mama had more babies. I mean, look at all that food!"

As Sachi made her way home, the birds were familiar with the path she took. But at one juncture, she turned in the opposite direction and kept going to the end of the alley. From here, she called out, "Mrs. Sado! Mrs. Sado!" And shortly, a black and white cat limped around the corner of the end building and slowly made her way to Sachi.

Mrs. Sado had mothered two of Sachi's best friends before they were trapped last year. No one ever knew what happened to them, as they were never seen again. In their mother's frantic search for them, she zig zagged across the streets, yelling out for her babies. A kid on a bike, not paying attention, ran over her hind leg and kept going. The leg never healed properly and now it was nearly impossible for Mrs. Sado to jump or run. After that, her will just left her. She gave up, stopped looking for her babies, and ate whatever crumbs were dropped from trash that was thrown out.

"Look what I've brought you. A baked chicken breast and some rice balls. Here, it's for you," Sachi said as she picked up the food in her mouth and laid it before Mrs. Sado.

As Mrs. Sado ate the delicious meal, Sachi stayed, talked to her, and protected her from hungry strays until only a few little bones remained on the ground. Then she put her forehead up against Mrs. Sado's, saying, "I will help you. I'll be back tomorrow with more food for you." With a final lick on Mrs. Sado's face, Sachi trotted down the alley back to the main street and turned in the direction of home.

She made one more stop. Mr. Goto had always been like a

grandfather to Sachi and her family. He was a lovely, old tomcat. Sachi found him under a bush in a side yard. When he saw her, he slowly stood up and walked towards her. He was so thin. Sachi hated seeing his hip bones stick out the way they did. "I have three fish and a boiled potato for you, Mr. Goto. Here, I'll sit with you and tell you a story about Taro."

The old cat looked at Sachi with such love and thanks. It saddened Sachi to think that she hadn't thought of this sooner. She vowed she'd keep him fed for as long as he lived.

With a lighter load to carry home, Sachi made it in no time, and her mother and Nori ran up to her, purring and laughing. They were always excited to see what new delights Sachi would serve up. Mika rolled on the ground, playing with a flower.

Sachi loved that she had the ability to provide for her family, and now others, in this way. And whenever she had this thought, she silently thanked Taro for having faith in himself to take the risk he took. Because in doing so, it created the opening that allowed Sachi to discover and fulfill her own potential as well.

The three birds were very taken by what they had seen. It was humbling, really. The better Sachi got at what she did, the more she had. And the more she had, the more she gave away.

Aja had taken the old carpenter's rule to measure twice and cut once. Everything fit Taro perfectly.

When she presented the garments to *Gennan* Roshi to inspect, *Aja* thanked him again for the honor of sewing Taro's clothing. Roshi smiled at the young woman. "You like Taro, don't you?"

"Yes, I do, Roshi," *Aja* replied.

Most of the monks favored Taro, but Roshi knew that *Aja* had a special bond with him. Considering this, he said, "How would you like to be Taro's attendant during his *tokudo*? You've earned the privilege."

This meant *Aja* would be up front with Roshi and have the honor of publicly dressing Taro in his robes. "Oh, Roshi, yes, yes! Absolutely! I would love that. Yes! Thank you, thank you!"

Roshi nodded. He liked her energy and wanted that kind of relationship up front when Taro was being ordained. She was the right person for the job.

All the monks at *Gakiji* loved *tokudo* ceremonies. They loved that the soon-to-be monk came out in what was considered underwear – the long, white kimono – and was literally dressed in front of everyone. It was incredible to see this concrete transformation into a monk, and *Gennan* Roshi was always brilliant in *tokudo* ceremonies.

But this ceremony was different. It would be the first one conducted outside, so all the creatures from the forest could attend. And Taro was, of course, a cat. It would be special and memorable in these ways. And now a date had been set. Taro's ordination ceremony would be conducted on the last Sunday of May. One week away.

In final preparation, Roshi called together *Aja*, the birds, and *Shōren*, a female monk who had studied with him for many years. Under a sugar maple next to the Temple gate's entrance, he started with the birds. He gave Hiroto another small pouch of powdered incense to take as an offering to Taro's mother so she would know the invitation was legitimate. He wanted Reiko to understand that she and her children would be welcomed as special guests to the Temple.

"Please invite the entire family and have them follow you back to *Gakiji*. They will stay here at the Temple with Taro. *Shōren* will accompany you to carry Mika back. Hopefully that will ease

Reiko's mind that Mika will arrive safely and be cared for during their stay."

The birds nodded and were set to take off when Roshi stopped them with one final request. "The date of the *tokudo* is one week from today. After you return with Taro's family, please make the announcement and extend the invitation to everyone in the forest. Let the old oak know and please tell the cherry trees that they will provide the coverage for the ceremony. And let Momo know, too. She will help spread the word. Ask her to invite Ratzitzu as her guest. Thank you. There will be a bowl of fresh blueberries waiting for you in the Maples when you return. See you back soon with the family."

And the birds headed out of the forest toward the village, chirping with excitement as *Shōren* happily shouted, "Hey! Wait up!"

Then Roshi turned his attention to *Aja* and the organization of the ceremony. "We can take everything we need outside," Roshi said. "That part of the ceremony is easy. But now it's time for you to practice dressing Taro. At least several times from start to finish so you both get the hang of it. It's one thing to dress yourself. Something entirely different to dress someone else. And a cat is, I don't know what. A cat. This has never been done before." Roshi's smile crinkled his eyes. "If you start practicing now, then the rest of your part is easy. Take care of Taro. That's all you need to do."

Aja was surprised at how far Taro's front legs, what she called his arms, could extend at right angles from his body. But she thought it looked unnatural, so decided to just have him hold his arms straight out. She said, "Taro, the sleeves of your *koromo* are very long and it can only be worn if you're upright. The design is taken from the Japanese Noh Theater. Here, I'll show you."

Taro sat up on his haunches, dressed in the white kimono

underwear with a smaller white shirt, the *jubon,* underneath. He curled his tail and tucked it neatly around him.

"Okay, Taro, now we're going to really practice," *Aja* said as she draped the black *koromo* over his back. "Now, hold your arms straight out and I'll put them through the sleeves for you. See how long the sleeves are? Keep your arms straight." Then she secured the *koromo* with ties and belted it. Lastly, she adjusted the sleeves by folding them back onto themselves so only his paws showed. "There. Now, bring your arms in and touch your paws together. Perfect!" And the sleeves of georgette fabric hung beautifully over Taro's body.

"How's it feel so far?" *Aja* asked.

"Weird. I never thought about having to wear clothes," Taro replied.

"Well, I'm sure you'll work something out with Roshi. Suspend judgment for now. Don't forget I have a jacket for you, too."

Taro smiled at his friend, so grateful she was going to be the one to dress him on Sunday.

"Now for the *rakusu*. Remember, this is the smaller version of your formal robe. Roshi will write your dharma name, the date and place of your *tokudo,* and stamp the *Gakiji* seal on the back. You won't be wearing it, so if Roshi gives it to you first, pass it on to me. No peeking. I will keep track of everything for you. All you have to do is be present."

Taro nodded his understanding.

"Okay, Taro, now I'm going to put the *rakusu* on you to make sure it fits. There's nothing on the back yet, so don't try and look for something that's not there! Here it comes, over your head. Okay, great. Perfect. Now take it off and hand it to me. That's right. Good." Taro completed that without any problem and *Aja* folded up his *rakusu* and put it to the side.

"Taro, the next thing is your robe, or *kesa,*" *Aja* said. "I've sewn it specifically for you so that you don't have to tie the knot. It's too complicated otherwise. Now, all we have to do is slip it over your head, adjust it a little, and voilà. One made to order kitty *kesa*! Now, can you stand up, please?"

When Taro stood up and the fabric fell into place, *Aja* was astonished at how he looked. "You're a beautiful Zen Buddhist cat, Taro.

"One more thing. You're also going to get a bowing mat because you must protect your *kesa* when you bow or sit down. But I've been told someone is going to manage the mat for you in the future. It will probably be whoever is next to you in the *zendo*. Sort of like how someone held your bowl for you when you went to the marketplace for *takuhatsu*.

"Now listen, Roshi will ask you to do three bows after you're fully dressed. Towards the end of the ceremony. The sleeves will probably fall down and you might get caught up in them. But that happens to all of us in the beginning. I'll teach you and you can practice. We've got the rest of this week," *Aja* said.

Taro had been with the monks long enough to see them bowing all the time. He asked, "*Aja*, why do the monks so often do three full bows in a row? Why not just one?"

"That's a very good question. The three bows represent humility, respect, and honor. They are strong aspects of our culture. It's quite simple yet profound, isn't it, mindfully doing the same thing three times. Yet, in the spirit of a complete action, each bow is done as if it were the very first time you have ever bowed. So it's not so simple."

"Yes. I never would have known. Thank you for enriching the act of bowing for me."

"Of course, then there are those who say we're so thick-headed we need to do things three times so the significance of what we're doing will sink in. Hahahahaha!"

Aja smiled at Taro. She couldn't get over what a treasure he was as she instinctively reached for him, then stopped herself. "Alright, let's take it from the top." And she started to undress him so they could do it all over again.

The birds took off one more time to return to the marketplace, mindful that *Shōren* was following on foot. This time, they decided to let Sachi grab her food, distribute it, then return home and eat before they approached the family. An after-meal invitation seemed the best way to ensure everyone was home and comfortable.

The wizardry of Sachi's moves was, as always, breathtaking, and the birds followed her as she left the marketplace and made her way first to Mrs. Sado and then to old Mr. Goto. Once home, the family converged, and they ate their meal in silent gratitude.

With the red-winged blackbird in front holding onto the incense pouch, the birds stood at the threshold and the other two chirped out, "Sachi, it's us. The birds from the forest where Taro lives in the monastery. May we come in? We have a gift for your mother and good news!"

"What? Mama! These are friends of Taro's from the forest. I've spoken with them before. It's okay to let them in. Okay?" Sachi asked her mother.

Reiko had already smelled the incense and remembered the anonymous gift earlier in the year. "Of course. Please come in."

The birds passed over the threshold and Hiroto dropped the incense pouch in front of Reiko. "A gift from *Gennan* Roshi. He sends his regards and an invitation to you and your family."

"An invitation?" asked Reiko as she picked up the incense. The girls gathered around her, Mika in Nori's arms.

"Yes! Taro is being ordained as a Zen Buddhist monk this Sunday. Roshi would like all of you to attend. You can follow us back to the Temple and stay there with Taro until the ceremony. Will you come? There's a really nice monk outside. Her name is *Shōren*. She's here to carry Mika to the Temple so the rest of you can travel freely. Hi, *Shōren*," Hiroto turned as he flapped his wings at her. *Shōren* waved back from outside and smiled.

"Taro? A Zen Buddhist monk?" Reiko said. "Oh, my goodness. Why, yes. Yes, of course! I never in a million . . ."

The birds tweeted loudly over her in excitement and joy for the family and their trip back to the forest.

"Before we go, there's something I have to do," Sachi said as she ran out.

"Wait! Sachi, where are you going? When will you be back?" Reiko called out, but Sachi was moving away too quickly.

Reiko turned to the birds, "My apologies. I don't know what that was all about, but we'll just have to wait for her to come back." The birds knew exactly where Sachi was going and reassured Reiko there was no hurry to leave.

While waiting for Sachi to return, Reiko took the incense and held it up to Nori and Mika. Little Mika was more interested in shadows on the wall, but Reiko and Nori regaled one another with stories of Taro. The birds flew up onto the farmhouse's rooftop and sunned themselves for as long as they could as *Shōren* lounged on a grassy patch under a tree, falling into a light sleep in the shade.

Gennan Roshi was prepared for Reiko and Taro's three sisters. The monks had cleared out a comfortable spot for them near the center of the Temple grounds, and Taro could stay with his family up until the night before his ceremony. There was plenty of food and the family would be treated with honor and respect. It was common for parents and siblings to attend major ceremonies conducted for their family members, but Taro's ordination was unprecedented.

Roshi thought about Ratzitzu. He expected the rat to behave himself, but always prepared for the worst.

When Sachi returned, her mother said, "What happened? Where were you? I was starting to worry."

Sachi smiled and said, "Trust me. It was important." Nothing more needed to be said. Sachi always kept her own counsel. Then she called her family outside and secured the screen against the threshold entrance.

Within five minutes, everyone headed towards the forest. The birds flew lower and slower than usual. Sachi ran around in circles under them, she had so much happy energy to burn. *Shōren* laughed as she carried little Mika, waving to the birds not to wait for her this time.

Within an hour, Reiko, Sachi, and Nori, led by the three birds, announced themselves at the Temple gate, which opened almost immediately. Everyone awaited the arrival of Taro's family.

Gennan Roshi approached them first. Seated on the ground with his legs tucked underneath him, he greeted Reiko and the girls and welcomed them to *Gakiji*. "It's a pleasure to have you as our guests. Everyone here is at your service. *Aja* is on her way right now. She will be the one who will watch over you and help you in any way. *Shōren* will be here shortly," Roshi said. "Her responsibility while you're here is to watch over Mika. She will bring Mika to the ceremony and hold her for you. Mika will be well taken care of, you have my word."

Shōren arrived then, almost as if on cue, laughing and cuddling Mika, who purred while she played with a leaf *Shōren* had picked up along the way.

Roshi continued, "The place we have for you is secured, so Mika can't wander off. Whenever you want help, just have Taro find *Shōren* and she will watch Mika for as long and as often as you'd like. That's what she's here to do for you."

Aja joined the group and knelt down next to Roshi. She loved Taro so much and could hardly believe she was in front of his family. The whole experience was unbelievable, and she fought back tears. "There's someone who has been waiting all day for you to come," she said.

Seconds later, Taro came charging full speed around the corner on all fours and ran straight to his mother. His force was so strong, he knocked her over and they rolled and purred until Sachi and Nori got such a kick out of it, they jumped the two of them and the family ended up one huge, tangled ball of multi-colored fur. Roshi, *Aja,* and *Shōren* laughed out loud as more monks came running out of the Temple to see what was so funny.

As the cats wound down, Roshi said, "*Aja,* why don't you and *Shōren* take Reiko and the family to their quarters. Taro, you go, too. You can all stay together for another few days. Meanwhile, welcome again. We're very happy to have you here. *Aja,* please escort the family and make sure they have food and water."

As the family left for their room, Roshi walked over to the birds who watched from the sugar maples near the entrance. "Because of you, Taro has everything he needs for Sunday. You are wonderful representatives of *Gakiji,* and I thank you for the role you took on with Taro and his family. I am indebted to you."

The birds had two more assignments to complete before the ceremony. They felt that the old oak and cherry trees already knew of the upcoming ceremony, but they were tasked with telling them, which is exactly what they did.

The oak tree shimmered in the sun's brilliance when the birds approached. Having already provided coverage for the Animal Blessing earlier, he believed Roshi's pick of the cherry trees was a perfect choice. He would listen in on the ordination and whatever he could not hear, he knew the wind would carry to him. He eagerly awaited the official ceremony.

The cherry trees humbly accepted the request to provide the canopy for Taro's *tokudo*. They spent the remainder of the week shedding dead leaves and flowers and pumping good energy into their root systems to ensure gorgeous blossoms. The honor was all theirs.

And finally, the birds went in search of Momo, who they found picking wildflowers near her home. "Momo!" they cried out as she looked up. She knew the birds never came to her for no reason. She wondered what they wanted her to do now.

They swooped in on her in a gentle way.

Hiroto said, "Oh, we're glad we found you. Taro's being ordained as a Zen Buddhist monk under the cherry trees on Sunday morning, and we need your help to spread the word!"

The flowers fell from Momo's grip. "What? This Sunday? Oh, my. It's less than a week away! Oh, oh, oh! Yes! Yes! I'll tell everyone. No one will want to miss this event," she said and clapped her paws.

"And there's one more thing," chirped Remi.

Momo stopped clapping and the smile left her face. *Now what? It was always something with these birds.*

"Roshi specifically asked us to ask you to invite Ratzitzu to the ceremony as your guest. Will you do it?"

What? Hell yeah! "Sure, yes, of course. Yes, yes. I will ask him. Of course, yes. I'll handle it. Yes, I'm on it."

Remi looked at her and thought, *I think she likes him . . . could that be possible?* "No, that was all Roshi asked. Bring him as your personal guest, and we'll see you Sunday morning. You'll have special guest seating. We'll show you when you get there. Thank you!"

And the birds flew off to the maples to feast on their blueberry snack. When finished, they finally roosted on a nearby low branch, reflecting on what a very full day it had been.

When Momo asked, "Ratzitzu, will you come with me to Taro's ordination ceremony on Sunday?" the invitation landed like a sucker punch to Ratzitzu's gut. It momentarily took his breath away. He panicked and needed several breaths of air before he could continue.

Watch Taro do what I wanted to do? Meet others? Leave the safety of my tunnel? Then in a moment of unusual self-reflection, he thought, *Okay, I can either go down the old path, or I could try something new here, I suppose. But I'm a hater not a lover. Yuck! What am I thinking?*

Momo stared up at him with shiny eyes that had begun to fill with tears. He had withdrawn into himself for a second, and the look in his eyes caused her to shake her head back and forth as she said, "I don't understand. I don't understand what happened. It was just an invitation."

And that unoffending head shake with her eyes brimming with tears was enough to begin to crack the spell Ratzitzu's former life held over him. In the space of all of Momo's goodness and kind heartedness, he allowed himself to feel the tension start to leave his body, his shoulders begin to relax. He took a big breath. "Yes. I can do that. Okay, okay, I'll go." *As long as you'll shield me from the crowd, I guess I can do it.* And that thought, even though it made him feel queasy, gave him just enough of a little bit of comfort.

Momo clasped her two tiny paws together, wiped her eyes, and started to applaud. Smiling, she said, "Thank you, Ratzitzu, thank you. It's in a few days, on Sunday morning. I'll come over here to get you, and we'll go together. See you then!"

And she skittered out of the tunnel before he could say anything else. Then she headed to the river to see what possibilities there might be for her hair.

The next several days that Taro spent with his family were like a dream. He took them around the *Gakiji* grounds, showed them where he worked in the pantries, demonstrated how to sit *zazen*, introduced them to the other monks, students, and forest creatures, and asked a million questions about what they were up to.

Late one afternoon, as Reiko, Nori, and Mika slept in the Temple's courtyard, Sachi told Taro about her extra giving to Mrs. Sado and old Mr. Goto. "When I sit with them, we talk about you all the time, Taro. They're so happy for you. I saw them just before we left to come here. They wanted you to know how proud of you they are and that they send their love and best wishes."

Taro was so taken by Sachi, never realizing she would expand her skills outside of the family. It moved him, thinking what she was capable of and what she had done.

"You inspired me to do this, Taro. When you took your place in the world, I realized that, in my own way, I could take my place in the world, too."

On Saturday afternoon, *Gennan* Roshi invited Reiko, the sisters, and Taro into his *dokusan* room for a small snack and some diluted tea water. He wanted the family to feel comfortable with him and the new role Taro was soon to take on as a Zen Buddhist monk.

About 30 minutes into this gathering, there was a knock on the door and *Daishin* entered. He said, "Excuse me. It's time for me to take Taro and begin preparation for tomorrow's ceremony. Taro, can you please come with me now?"

Taro licked his mother and his sisters several times and gave Sachi a gentle, loving punch on the shoulder as he stood up. Then he bowed to his teacher and left with *Daishin* to start the next chapter of his life.

Daishin led Taro to a room with a connecting bathroom where eight of the most senior male monks sat in two rows across from one another. A candle and incense were already lit on a small altar. The room felt like a cocoon, which was the intention.

Daishin motioned to Taro to take the empty seat in one row, and *Daishin* took the seat across from Taro.

Then he began, "Taro, we've never done a *tokudo* with a cat before. The evening before *tokudo* is typically used for head shaving, bathing, and *zazen*. At this time, Roshi has waived the head shaving. He felt the shaved head symbolism of re-birth would be lost unless we shaved you completely down. And this will not do. But, we will bathe you and tomorrow when you're given your dharma name, the old Taro will stay in the past where he belongs, and you will be born into a new future to take out into the world. After we leave tonight, you will stay in this room until the ceremony starts tomorrow. I'll be back in the morning to help you get ready. Do you have any questions?"

It was bad enough for Taro to think about having all his fur shaved off but when he said, "A bath?" *Daishin* and the other monks burst out laughing. They weren't always serious. "The water is warm and we won't dunk your head. Promise. It's not a baptism. It's just a bath. You'll be fine," *Daishin* assured him as all the monks continued to smile.

And with that, one of the monks drew a warm bath for Taro. He placed him gently into the water and started chanting along with the remaining monks kneeling around the tub. They each scrubbed him with a very nice, clean-smelling soap and rinsed him well. When they finished, the largest monk took Taro out of the tub, drew off the excess water, and placed him snugly in an oversized towel. A few more towel rubs and the monk exchanged it for a dry towel. *Daishin* told Taro to face the altar and mentally begin to prepare for his ceremony. He said, "I'll be here in the morning to help dress you and escort you to your *tokudo*. Stay in *zazen*. Until then, good night."

Taro, left alone in the room, stared at the flickering candle and let his mind drift back to the first night he'd sat outside the Temple gate in the cold. He had been so frightened then. He had doubted his future. He had risked his family and his life, with his one request. *I want to train with Roshi.* And he didn't even know what that meant back then. Now, on the eve of his ordination, just thinking those words filled Taro with strength and faith. So many people and forest creatures had come forward to help him, to train and teach him, to encourage him. All their actions were unique contributions that moved him toward this moment. And there were dark forces, too. Good and evil always co-existed. One could not arise without the other. Ratzitzu was a powerful teacher who stretched Taro in ways no one else could have. He was now so grateful for the rat and deeply appreciative of Roshi's wisdom to keep Ratzitzu at the Temple. Thinking of all those who took part in his development, he wondered, *How can I ever repay even one of them?*

As Taro fell into a peaceful sleep, his last thoughts drifted to what the ordination would hold for him, what name Roshi envisioned, and what that possibility would mean for his future.

CHAPTER Sixteen

MOMO WAS SO excited when Sunday finally arrived. Her nervous energy woke her up early, and she dashed around in circles before she calmed down. Not only would Taro be ordained today, but Ratzitzu had agreed to be her special guest at the ceremony. Her little paws instantly flew to the top of her head. *Oh, no! My hair!* She dashed to the river. Maybe something had changed overnight. And of course, it hadn't, as she saw in her reflection in the river. In fact, her tuft was unusually sticky-outy this morning.

The three birds chirped and sang as they perched on a tree branch that stuck up just a few inches above the river, making it the perfect place to dip in for a bath. They were preparing for Taro's ceremony, as well. First a bath, then they would preen their feathers.

Catching a movement out of the corner of his eye, Hiroto looked up and saw Momo several hundred yards away. Something didn't look right. He flapped his wings sharply to silence the other two. "Be still! I think Momo is upset. Let's see what's going on." And he flew off as the other two hurried to catch up with him.

Momo saw the birds coming in her direction. *Oh, no. No. Please, no. Not now. Not today. I can't do anything for you. My hair is a mess. Leave me alone.* Looking up at them, she waved, "Oh, hi. Hi! How's it going? Good to see you!"

Hiroto landed and got very close to her. "What's wrong? You don't look so great."

"I know, I know. I know. It's just that . . . look at my hair!" Momo wailed as she reached up to the top of her head. "I just wanted it to look nice for once. Just once. That's all I wanted." Lowering her paws, little tears fell from her eyes as her tuft split in several different directions.

"Oh, it's not so . . ." Genji started to say as Remi brushed him aside with her wing and hopped forward.

"Momo, we're going to fix this for you."

And she began to direct the two males. "Go get those wildflowers over there. The white and pink ones. No, not those. They're too heavy. Over there. And there. Grab the tops of those tall purple ones. And bring some of the yellow buttercups, too."

Hiroto and Genji flew all about, dropping flowers, grass, and leaves in a pile in front of Remi, who had already begun to sort everything. Finally, she said, "Okay! That's enough. Now come over here and do exactly what I tell you to do."

Under Remi's critical eye and careful instructions, Hiroto and Genji began to weave a bouquet of wildflowers and leaves, eventually using Momo's own tuft to secure the flower crown to the top of her head.

Finally, Remi said, "Okay, you can stop." Hopping back, she regarded Momo from top to bottom and nodded, "Momo, you look beautiful."

When Momo saw herself reflected in the river's water, her little paws immediately flew together in prayerful thanks to the birds. She felt so lovely. After another moment's gaze of herself in the water, she said, "It's funny. The thing I hated the most turned out to be the thing that I needed more than anything." And she happily scuttled off to pick up Ratzitzu so they would arrive at the ceremony on time, her "thank you, thank you, thank you" to the birds trailing behind her.

Aja had the honor of being Taro's attendant and dressing him during the ceremony. This was a privilege she did not take lightly. Setting up the ceremonial table under the cherry trees, she felt a powerful sense of pride in Taro's accomplishments. Her eyes began to sting with tears.

She covered the low table with a purple cloth and smoothed it out, slowly running her hands over the silk fabric. It brought back memories of her own *tokudo* and how her family had eventually come to accept the choice she had made.

Knowing what Roshi would need to conduct the ceremony, *Aja* started to organize everything on the table. She placed the *hako* directly in the center of the table. With its mound of powdered incense fluffed high for easy pinching on one side and the tamped down ash as smooth as glass on the other, she gently placed an unlit charcoal briquette directly in the center of the ash. During the *tokudo*, placing the powdered incense onto the lit charcoal was a ceremonial tradition. The smoke coming off the powdered incense would be used to sanctify. *Aja* could never get enough of the smell and was happy there were so many things that would need to be incensed today.

She put lilacs in a ceramic vase that had been given to Roshi as a gift from the family of a departing monk. Then she picked up Roshi's liturgy book with both hands and looked down at it. It was the embodiment of his very essence. It contained every word he needed to say, every action he needed to take to keep the dharma alive as he formally passed on his wisdom and teachings. Even though *Aja* knew Roshi could do any ceremony in the book by heart, this book kept the record of everything of value he had to give. The pages had been turned back and forth for decades and many were creased, torn, or dog-eared. She loved that there were notes written in the margins and left-over papers with important information like the names of family members or quotes he wanted to add. One day, she knew he would pass this liturgy book on to the next Abbot of *Gakiji*.

Respectfully placing the book on the right side of the table, she carefully cleaned his reading glasses and placed them on top of his book, just the way she knew he liked them. She put a white candle behind the book, merely as a symbol. Finally, she placed a small brass cup of water with a pine bough draped over the top in front of the *hako*.

Aja then took Roshi's cushion and squared it to the table so he would be looking out at the assemblage. On the other side of the table, she carefully arranged Taro's cushion across from Roshi's, and then her own, which faced Taro's family. Guests of honor have the best seats in a ceremony, and Reiko and the girls would be seated right up-front facing Taro, so they could see everything. With luck, Mika would be sleeping securely in *Shōren's* lap.

Aja put everything Taro would need to complete his ceremony in a perfectly ordered, neat pile next to her mat. Having completed her task, she humbly thanked the cherry trees, bowed, and returned to the Temple.

A good teacher knows that wherever there is great evil, there is always potential for great goodness. Roshi had faith in Ratzitzu, although it was a newfound faith. But since Roshi didn't want anything to upset Taro's ceremony, he thought it prudent to strategically place Ratzitzu's seat next to *Shōren's* and have Momo border him on the other side. The three birds would be perched on a cherry branch directly above Ratzitzu's head. *Aja's* seat at the low table in the front placed her looking in Ratzitzu's direction. Once that was done, Roshi let go of any further thoughts of seating arrangements. Whatever happened, happened.

Ratzitzu felt he had spent too much time getting ready, but it was hard to stop. He had chewed down several sticks already that morning, slicked all the kinks out of his whiskers, and raked a paw through the top of his head so many times he thought his fur must look a little flat for all that effort. Then he heard Momo at the entrance to his tunnel.

When she arrived, he blinked twice, stared at her, and thought *Wow, I don't know how you did that, but you look cute. Maybe even kind of hot.*

Momo, ever self-conscious, gave a little squeak. "What? What's wrong?" she asked, believing that if someone stared at her for too long, there was probably something wrong either with her or her hair.

"Nothing's wrong," he said. "Uh, you look, uh . . . pretty good, I guess."

And Momo accepted that as a compliment, even though she felt she looked better than just *pretty good*. "Come on, Ratzitzu! Are you ready? We have to hurry so we aren't late for the ceremony. We have good seats waiting for us. Come on!" And Momo flew out of the tunnel on a burst of nervous energy, kicking up dirt behind her.

Ratzitzu picked up another stick and ran out behind her, trying to avoid getting dirt in his eyes. At least gnawing on a stick would give him something to do in case he ran out of things to say.

Everyone in the forest was in a festive mood. When word got out about Taro's ordination and that they were all included in the ceremony, the animals started to make their way to the cherry trees in droves. Even those who had never formally met Taro wanted to support him for what he had accomplished. It was an honor to witness his ordination.

The three birds flew back and forth over the crowd in long arcs, chirping and tweeting, encouraging everyone to keep moving forward. They finally landed on top of a low cherry branch. The leaves fluttered and a few blossoms dropped on Reiko and Sachi, who had just arrived and taken their seats. Nori was a little behind her family, making sure Mika wasn't too much of a handful for *Shōren*. Once she was happy that Mika was resting comfortably, Nori quickly took her seat next to Sachi and snuggled in beside her mother.

Ratzitzu had only one focus. He kept his attention on Momo's hair flowers and wondered how she got them to stay that way. Everyone was a mystery to him, but females were especially perplexing.

By 9:00 a.m. the body of monks had arrived and everyone was seated. The briquette in the *hako* had been lit and, as in the Animal Blessing ceremony, it was one junior monk's only responsibility to mind the heated charcoal to keep the forest safe from any potential sparks.

Gennan Roshi made his entrance through the middle of the crowd. He bowed, then walked around the table and sat on his cushion. He gazed out at the animals and all his monks, then dropped a pinch of incense onto the briquette. Thin trails of smoke rose up.

Aja sat in her seat, perpendicular to Roshi.

Now everyone waited for Taro.

Meanwhile, *Daishin* had entered Taro's room, where he sat waiting.

Daishin said, "I brought a vegetable brush to run through your fur, just in case we need it. It's clean. We don't have combs or anything like that here, you know, because most of us don't have hair, being mostly bald and all." And he started to brush Taro along his back, down his sides, and under his chin and tail. It felt heavenly, and Taro purred and purred. Who cared if the brush was meant for turnips and potatoes? It was a most generous thought on *Daishin's* part.

Then *Daishin* told Taro to stand up to be dressed in his white kimono. The monk's underwear. He said, "You'll have to present yourself standing up. The kimono wasn't designed for someone walking on all fours." When Taro stood and *Daishin* placed a stretchy belt around Taro's belly to keep the kimono secured, everything fell into place. "It's perfect," Daishin said. "*Aja* did a beautiful job. Are you ready to go?"

Taro nodded and *Daishin* led him out to the cherry trees. Taro heard a *taiko* drum beating in the background.

As they drew closer to Roshi, Taro felt the energy and excitement. He saw little babies jumping up and down, reaching out to touch him. He heard one little animal say, "Oh, Mama, he looks just like a Zen angel."

Up ahead, he saw his mother, Sachi, and Nori. He felt a deep love for them. He noticed that little Mika was fast asleep in *Shōren's* lap and was thankful his sister wasn't awake and wiggling to be set free. He saw the twins, Ben and Ren, and was amazed at how mature they had become, now sporting beautiful velvet antlers. They majestically bowed to him. Taro looked up and saw the birds, who had been his constant companions. They waited for him.

Momo, with beautiful flowers arranged in a crown on her head, sat next to Ratzitzu. Taro almost dared to think they looked like a handsome couple. In the end, who would have thought Ratzitzu would have ever come out to witness something he had once coveted so fiercely for himself.

And then, out of nowhere, the now fully grown hawk Taro had seen the first time he'd entered the forest in the daytime, appeared. Once again, he angled his wings in greeting.

Taro stopped and saluted him, as he had years before. The hawk swooped down and flew three grand rotations around Taro's head before climbing back to the heavens. A white feather fell from its tail and slowly fluttered toward the earth. Everyone was awed into silence.

Daishin caught the feather from the sky and watched the hawk depart, then leaned down to Taro. He held the feather out in front of Taro for him to see. "The hawk is telling you that your life is about to take a turn. Soon you will be called to your purpose. And it will be supported by the heavens," he said before he turned and continued to lead Taro to Roshi.

When Taro saw Roshi up ahead at the end of the path, his image brought Taro home to the center of his being. Fully relaxed and grounded, Taro was ready for Roshi to take him to the next level of what was possible for his future. A future Taro knew Roshi considered as having already been fulfilled upon.

When *Daishin* got to the ceremonial table, he handed the feather to Roshi and stepped aside. There was one final, thundering strike on the *taiko* as Taro bowed to Roshi.

Daishin motioned to Taro to approach his mother before he said, "With all your heart, with all your love, and with all your might, please make three full bows to your mother and to the memory of your father."

Taro walked over and stood directly in front of his mother. He lowered his body and forehead to the ground. Raising his paws above his head, Taro bowed three times, all the while thinking, *I love you, Mama. Thank you so much for being here. I love you, Papa. Please be proud of me.*

Reiko was overcome. She had no idea this would happen. Nori moved even closer to her. Then Taro turned back to *Daishin*.

Motioning towards Roshi, *Daishin* said, "With all your heart, with all your love, with all your might, please make three full bows to your preceptor, *Gennan* Roshi."

Taro poured his full devotion into this action. He owed an enormous debt of gratitude to Roshi and showed this by staying with his head down on the ground for a beat longer than usual. After the completion of his third bow, Roshi motioned Taro to sit down on his cushion.

Then in a loud voice, *Daishin* turned toward the assemblage. "Honored family, friends, and guests. I respectfully announce to everyone that the Ordination Ceremony for Taro will now begin."

Ratzitzu was daydreaming. He wondered what would have happened if he had managed to stay with *Ekō* Roshi. What his own ceremony would have looked like. He knew there would have been no family to celebrate with him. And probably none of *Ekō* Roshi's monks would have cared that much about him to have felt any joy or happiness about his ordination. He figured their attendance would have been out of obligation to the tradition and respect for their relationship with Roshi, rather than have anything to do with him. Those thoughts saddened him.

He had spent so many years going unnoticed, he was good at making it seem like it didn't matter. But it did. When the truth was told, deep inside he had been very lonely. He knew it was an unfulfilled way to live, and it left him with a painful ache. He instinctively put his paw on his stomach.

"Are you alright? Is everything okay?" Momo asked.

"Yes," said Ratzitzu, removing his paw. "Everything is fine now."

Bitterness and jealousy had begun to loosen its grip on him, and he found he could watch the ceremony with greater ease. More importantly, he knew there would have been no Momo had he stayed with *Ekō* Roshi. She was the first friend he ever had. And because of her, he found that other things were becoming more important to him.

Roshi dropped extra pinches of incense onto the charcoal when he wanted to punctuate something of importance. Now, through the smoke, he said, "Taro, think right now with gratitude toward your parents and thank them for having given you this life. Consider carefully what your family has done for you, and what this beautiful forest, the trees, the rocks and flowers, and your friends have given to you."

To give Taro some time for reflection, Roshi dropped one more pinch of powdered incense for effect and waited. As he did this, Taro thought, *All the different kinds of animals and things exist freely and happily together here. There's a flock of birds looking down on us who first encouraged me to approach the Temple gate and then went on to recover me at my lowest point. A human is ordaining me who, less than two years ago, rejected me. I was so afraid that gate would never open to me. The trees talk, and people and animals communicate back and forth. I almost killed little Momo. But now look at her, so happy and pretty, sitting next to Ratzitzu, who almost killed me. My mother has forgiven me, and Sachi has gone on to give her gift away, benefitting so many others.* In that moment, Taro was filled with unspeakable joy. Rather than assume he knew or controlled anything, he vowed he would let all things of the world present themselves on their own terms.

Roshi picked up Taro's black outerwear, his *koromo,* rotated it three times in a clockwise direction over the smoke from the incense, and handed it to Taro. Taro accepted it and gave it to *Aja,* the way they had practiced. Then Taro stood on his hind legs and extended his arms out as *Aja* kneeled behind him with his *koromo.* Draping it over his body, she began to dress him. She tied and belted the garment, rolled the sleeves back onto themselves, and Taro sat back down on his haunches.

Roshi repeated the incensing ritual and handed Taro his lineage chart that documented the "bloodline" of succession from the original Buddha, through *Gennan* Roshi, to Taro. That was followed by Buddha's eating bowl, which *Aja* neatly put in the pile for Taro.

And then Roshi incensed Taro's black *kesa*, or Buddha's robe. *Aja* draped it over Taro's left side, and his dressing was complete.

Before moving to the final part of the ceremony, Roshi asked *Aja* to hand him Taro's *rakusu*. He opened it, nodded, then folded it back up, and rotated it over the smoke. Then he handed it back to *Aja*, who gently placed it in Taro's pile.

Finally, *Aja* handed Roshi a document in an origami envelope that everyone was waiting for. Now Taro's dharma name would be revealed. With another pinch of incense on the charcoal, Roshi rotated the envelope through the smoke three times. Then he took out the paperwork and read what he had written. *Aja* bowed her head as a tear trickled down her cheek. She sat in anticipation.

"Hmmm. Dharma name for Taro," Roshi said, folding the paper and placing it back in its origami envelope. He handed it to *Aja*, sprinkled more incense, and began.

"Taro, the dharma name I have chosen for you is the essence of life itself. This name embodies all of the natural world and all of the animal kingdom. It is who you are. It is the purpose you sought and have worked so hard for. You are no longer a little cat in the forest. Everything between heaven and earth, you are the force of *Nature*. You are ***Shizen***!" Roshi shook his fist and said the dharma name with great passion and emphasis.

"The hawk has already spoken to you," Roshi said as he incensed the feather three times, then handed it to *Aja* to place at the top of Taro's things. "His arrival was a sign that you are exactly where you need to be to fulfill your purpose."

Roshi continued, "This *tokudo* acknowledges the evolutionary shift that has taken place, where animals have begun to evolve. With every evolution, morality also has to develop along with a higher set of values beyond that of mere survival. You are at the tip of that spear. You are being called to lead the animals."

Ratzitzu's mouth fell open. Momo brought her little paws to her chest with a gasp, and Taro's mother sat wide-eyed in stunned silence. Sachi turned and high-fived everyone around her and would have kept going if Nori hadn't poked her.

For Taro, though, the news was too much to absorb. He couldn't make sense of what Roshi was saying to him. He started to panic. He didn't know what he should be doing. What was it exactly Roshi had said? Taro imagined failure all around him, remembering the vegetable garden. But then he thought of the hawk and the gift of his feather. And that image brought a profound peace to Taro, allowing space to breathe. And in that space, his fear began to drop away. Nothing had to happen in this moment, or even today. Everything would come together in due time.

Roshi sprinkled a few more pinches of incense into the *hako* and watched as the smoke rose up. He loved doing that. "This *tokudo* is not about you, *Shizen*. It's not personal. This is about the evolution of the animal kingdom into a realm of knowing and being that has never been seen or thought of before. And what comes along with this is the responsibility to ensure the forest and her animals continue to exist and thrive alongside humans." Roshi looked out and the cherry trees shimmered. Pink blossoms floated down on everyone.

"Along with the old oak tree," Roshi said, "comes the privilege of being a steward of the forest and protector of the animal kingdom.

"You've been chosen. The question before you is, do you accept the responsibility of this leadership and all it involves? It's a choice only you can make."

Shizen looked at *Gennan* Roshi. It was exactly as *Aja* had said. A vision to live into that was greater than who he thought himself to be. He had no idea what to think, what to do, or how to be this leader. But he knew he wouldn't have to do it on his own. So many people and animals were behind him. Even the trees and plants. He was not in this world alone. He would be the bridge between the Temple and the forest, and maybe even beyond.

"Yes, Roshi. I accept," *Shizen* said.

Roshi nodded and sprinkled more powdered incense into the *hako*. "Three bows, please. Oh, wait! One more thing." The entire forest held its breath.

"There is one more thing." Roshi looked over at Reiko, smiled, then returned his attention to *Shizen*. "*Aja* sewed your button into the back of your *rakusu*. It's in a safe and sacred place now."

Roshi sprinkled a final pinch of incense into the *hako*. "Three bows, please."

Glossary

Aja – ***Ah*** *dzah*– one of Roshi's monks and friend to Taro
Daishin – ***Dī*** *shin* – *Gennan* Roshi's attendant
Dokusan – ***Dō*** *ku san* – private interview or time with a Roshi
Ekō – *Echo* – Abbot of Dragon Gate Zen Buddhist Temple
Fusatsu – *Fu* ***saht*** *su* – renewal of the monks' vows ceremony
Gakiji – *Gah kē* ***gē*** – Temple name of the Hungry Ghost Zen Buddhist Temple
Gasshō – *Gah* ***shō*** – palms together signifying non-duality
Genji – **Ghen** gē – male cardinal
Gennan – ***Ghen*** *nan* – Abbot of the Hungry Ghost Zen Buddhist Temple
Hako – ***Hah*** *kō* – box for powdered incense
Hiroto – Hē **rō** tō – red-winged blackbird
Kanshō – ***Kahn*** *shō* – small bell rung by student prior to entering *dokusan* with a Roshi
Kesa – ***Kā*** *sah* – the monk's robe
Kōan – ***Kō*** *ahn* – an illogical story or riddle to provoke enlightenment
Kogen – ***Kō*** *ghen* – *Ekō* Roshi's attendant
Oryoki – *O rē* ***o*** *kē* – the practice of accepting just enough food
Rakusu – ***Rah*** *ku su* – small version of a monk's robe

Ratzitzu – Rat **zit** su –the rat who fights against Taro; the story's antagonist
Reiko – **Rā** koh – Taro's mother
Remi – **Rheh** mē – female cardinal
Rohatsu – Rō ***hot*** *su* – Buddha's enlightenment *sesshin*
Ryoban – ***Rē*** *ō bahn* – a row of mats facing one another for senior monks
Ryumonij – Rē oo ***mahn*** *gē* – Temple name of the Dragon Gate Temple
Sachi – **Sah** chē – Taro's sister
Samue – ***Sam*** *oo ā* – short jacket worn for work practice
Sesshin – Seh ***shin*** - intensive practice period
Shizen – ***Shē*** *zen* – dharma name meaning *Nature*
Takuhatsu – Tah ku ***hot*** *su* – reciprocal act of giving blessings for food and money
Taro – **Tah** rō – main character; the story's protagonist
Tokudo – ***Tō*** *ku dō* – monk ordination ceremony
Zazen - Zah ***zen*** - to sit; Zen meditation
Zendo – ***Zen*** *dō* – room where the monks perform *zazen*

Acknowledgments

To the *Gakiji Hungry Ghost Zen Buddhist Temple* Sangha. Many, many years ago, we practiced, trained, and played together in Santa Monica, CA. Some of the richest experiences I had with you have been written into Taro's story. I will never forget that time in my life.

To Nicolee *Jikyo* McMahon, Roshi. I owe you a debt of gratitude as my *tokudo* (ordination) preceptor and for training me for so long during high and low times in my life. Your ideas on spreading the Dharma in new and creative ways have always been your magic.

To Laurie Horowitz. You are an incredible mentor. As my original writing coach, you were with me from the conception of *Taro the Zen Cat* through to the very end, and way beyond. Thank you for all the feedback you gave me, going over and over these pages with me for so long, teaching and supporting me. I have learned so much from you about the technique and art of writing.

To my Los Angeles writing group — Tamara Holub, Chris Richardson, Jan Shure-Hurwitz, Lily Houston, Sheelagh O'Connor, Katie Saunders, Jason Meisler, Shelli Margolin-Meyer, Lené Amalfi, and Jennifer Clay. Every single one of you influenced and shaped my writing. You can't begin to imagine the value of your contributions. Thank you for noticing the small things. You live in Taro.

To my beta readers — Bea Fulton, Jeri Dwyer, Natalie DeJarlais, Jill Jordan, Ren'e Fedyna, and Diane A. Curran. Thank you from a place deeper than the bottom of my heart for the time and attention you gave so willingly. The questions you had and the comments you made were spot on and enriched the story of Taro's journey a hundredfold.

To my Acorn Publishing team — Holly Kammier, Jessica Therrien, and Evelyn Lawhorn. With profound gratitude, I acknowledge all the work you did to maneuver me through the wondrous, mysterious waters of publishing.

To Laura Taylor, my exceptional content editor at Acorn Publishing. Every grammatical error you corrected, every suggestion you offered, absolutely everything was done with such grace and respect. I am forever grateful for your skill and clarity. Thank you beyond words for elevating my work.

To Alberto Soriano, creator of my book cover and master watercolorist extraordinaire. You translated my ideas onto paper with professionalism, ease, and imagination. You brought to life exactly what I was thinking as Taro entered the magical forest. Thank you, thank you for being my teacher and my friend.

A Alberto Soriano, creador de la portada de mi libro y maestro extraordinario de la acuarela. Usted ha plasmado mis ideas en el papel con profesionalidad, facilidad e imaginación. Ha dado vida exactamente a lo que yo pensaba cuando Taro entró en el bosque mágico. Gracias, gracias por ser mi maestro y mi amigo.

And to my muses, Oliver and Beck. Oliver who inspired Taro, and Beck who inspired Sachi, even though you're a male. It's okay, buddy, it all worked out. I would look at you two and always be encouraged to keep going, to write more. You are such sweet cats. I love you both so much.

About the Author

The day after Jennifer J. Hunter completed her dissertation, she experienced empty-nest writer's syndrome, joined a writing group in Los Angeles, and never looked back.

An avid lover of animals, she has been a Zen Buddhist priest for decades. Much of what she has learned in life she would rather forget; however, two bits of wisdom shine through:

1) Appreciate how extraordinary your ordinary life is.

2) Be kind to animals. They are often our best friends and teachers and deserve our kindness.

Jennifer holds an MA in Speech-Language Pathology, an MSW in Clinical Social Work, and a PhD in Leadership and Change. Taro the Zen Cat was born in her kitchen one afternoon while she was eating a frozen blueberry yogurt bar.

She lives high up in the Andes in Cuenca, Ecuador, with her two best buddies, Oliver and Beck, who inspired the characters Taro and Sachi.

About the Artist

Claudio Alberto Soriano Vitorino is a prominent artist who moved from Peru to Ecuador 30 years ago. Throughout his career, his artistic exhibitions have been exceptionally well received and he has distinguished himself in the master mediums of watercolor, acrylics, and oil with remarkable expertise and imagination. He created the magical cover of Taro the Zen Cat, an original watercolor, in his studio at idiomART in the heart of Old Town in Cuenca, Ecuador.

www.ingramcontent.com/pod-product-compliance
Lightning Source LLC
Chambersburg PA
CBHW020558310726
48979CB00008B/1254/J
* 9 7 9 8 8 8 5 2 8 0 7 4 7 *